S0-ARC-016

"The Roger Hallen Show?" Daniel Brown was in his shirt sleeves at the kitchen table. His dark, muscular arms were folded across his chest. "She going to sing or something?"

"No, she's going to talk about what it's like being one of the most exciting young models in America." Loretta Barrett stirred her coffee by moving the spoon quickly at the top of the cup. "I'm sure he'll ask her how she manages to balance her schoolwork with her modeling, that kind of thing. It'll be wonderful for her."

"And how much she get for being on his show?" Crystal's father asked.

"Five hundred dollars," Crystal said. "How do I look?"

"That's all?" Daniel turned his head sideways.

"What they pay is the absolute minimum they can get away with," Loretta said. "The prestige is supposed to be payment enough."

"Do you really have to work tonight, Daddy?" Crystal asked. "You could come see me."

WALTER DEAN MEYERS is the author of many books, including *Motown and Didi*, winner of the Coretta Scott King Award, *Hoops*, and *The Outside Shot*. All are available in Laurel-Leaf editions. Mr. Meyers grew up in Harlem and now lives in Jersey City, New Jersey.

Crystal

Walter Dean Myers

Published by
Dell Publishing
a division of
Bantam Doubleday Dell Publishing Group, Inc.
666 Fifth Avenue
New York, New York 10103

The trademark Laurel-Leaf Library® is registered in the U.S. Patent
and Trademark Office.

The trademark Dell® is registered in the U.S. Patent and Trademark
Office.

ISBN: 0-440-20538-7

RL: 4.9

Reprinted by arrangement with Viking Penguin, Inc.

Printed in the United States of America

January 1990

10 9 8 7 6 5 4 3 2

RAD

To Spencer Shaw, who has been a friend to me and, more important, to children's literature.

Crystal

1

Jee-sus called my na-ame
Early in the morning

CRYSTAL BROWN ROCKED WITH THE BEAT AS SHE STOOD in the front row of the gospel choir. Her best friend, Pat, was leading what had to be the last song of the morning. Victory Tabernacle's air-conditioning, which had never worked that well, was down again, and droplets of sweat ran down Crystal's body under the gray-and-gold robes.

I heard him call my na-ame
Early in the morning

Crystal watched as Sister Mason lifted a large brown hand to chase a fly buzzing around her newly straightened hair, the tambourine in her other hand never missing a beat as it slapped against her thigh.

Jee-sus called my na-ame
Early in the morning

3

Reverend Curry was already on his feet and making his way to the pulpit as the congregation ended the song in joyful unison.

And I-I will fol-ol-low Him

"Praise His holy name." Reverend Curry's deep voice filled the church.

There was a chorus of amens as the congregation responded.

"Before we leave this morning"—Reverend Curry patted the perspiration from his forehead—"let us thank the Lord one more time for the blessings He has bestowed on us. Let us bow our heads in prayer one more time, even though we know that we cannot thank Him enough. . . ."

More amens followed and Sister Jenkins raised her hands to the heavens, the nearly white palms contrasting sharply with the rich darkness of her face.

"Lord, walk with us today wherever we may go. . . ." Reverend Curry's eyes were closed. "Keep our feet from straying and our minds on higher ground. . . ."

Crystal glanced at the big clock in the back of the church. It was twelve-thirty, she would have a good hour to get to the studio.

"Let men walk in love with their wives and let parents walk in love with their children. . . . Let us feel Your presence no matter how high we stand or how low. . . ."

Crystal glanced over at Loretta and saw the only White woman in the church sitting with her head bowed.

"Let us understand that there is no greater gift in the world

4

than Your sweet mercy . . . and no greater words in all the world than these we offer today."

There was a shuffling about as the entire congregation stood.

"Our Father, Who art in heaven . . . Hallowed be Thy name . . . Thy kingdom come . . . Thy will be done . . ."

"You going to do some modeling today?" LuWanda Feelings combed her hair out in front of the mirror in the dressing room as she talked. "I saw that lady out there."

"I'm going to meet a photographer," Crystal said.

"Reverend Curry say anything about you working on Sunday?"

"I told you I wasn't working," Crystal said. She hung up her robe and put it on the rack. "I'm just going to meet a photographer."

"How come you can't meet him during the week?" Lu-Wanda asked.

"Why you got to ask Crystal so many questions about what she's doing?" Carrie Smith stood with her hands on her hips. "What she does is between her and the Lord. And she don't need you looking out for her, and I know the Lord don't."

"I was just asking!" LuWanda gave Carrie a look, then thought better of challenging the older girl. "I was just wondering what a model be doing, that's all."

Crystal watched LuWanda walk off and catch up with some of the women in the senior choir.

"That girl ain't gonna die no natural death," Carrie said. "She gonna *nosey* on out the world!"

"She's okay," Crystal said.

"What's okay about her?" Carrie was straightening her dress in the mirror. "Her sister told me that when they came to shoot that commercial, she stayed up half the night putting relaxer in her hair."

"She did?"

"Yeah, she did," Carrie said. "And if she thought she could have been picked to go downtown as a model like you, she would have stayed up the other half, too."

"I've got to get out of here!" Crystal looked at her watch.

"Crystal, if you meet Bill Cosby or somebody like that, you be sure to let me be the first to know about it. You hear me, girl?"

"I hear you, Carrie."

"And don't forget that Sister Curry wanted to see you."

Loretta Barrett met Crystal at the front door of the church and walked with her to her car. Carol Brown, Crystal's mother, was already there, talking with Mother Glover and nervously glancing toward the front entrance of the church.

"How did you like the services?" Crystal asked Loretta as they neared the agent's car.

"They were lovely and too long," Loretta said. "It's the same in every church. They're like football games, you can never tell when one of them ends and the next one begins."

"Child, you sure are growing." Mother Glover put her hand on Crystal's shoulder. "How you get to be so big so soon?"

"I don't know." Crystal shrugged. Out of the corner of her eye she saw Loretta open the car door.

"How you doing in school?" Mother Glover tilted her head

6

sideways and looked at Crystal. "You still getting them A's and B's?"

"Yes, ma'am," Crystal said, knowing that her grades were mostly C's.

"Well, you just keep on getting them," Mother Glover said.

"Honey, I'm not going down to the studio with you today," Carol Brown said to her daughter. "I've got a terrible headache. Why don't you just go on with Loretta."

"Mama, I didn't know you had a headache," Crystal said. "You take anything for it?"

"I'm going up and lie down until your father gets home," Mrs. Brown said. "You'd better be getting along now."

There was something in her mother's eyes that bothered Crystal. If there had been more time, a few minutes even, she would have asked about it. Instead, she found herself smiling, kissing her mother quickly on the cheek, and sliding into the car next to Loretta.

Loretta pulled the steel-gray Chrysler away from the curb and slowly through the crowd coming from Crystal's church, Victory Tabernacle, toward Marcy Avenue. There was a stick-ball game on Marcy, and Loretta had to wait until a skinny brown-skinned boy, his hair braided tightly against his head, went around the bases before she could continue.

"Did I tell you we almost didn't do the commercial here because of Jim Aronson?"

"No." Crystal looked at the dark-haired woman next to her. "I thought he was the one—"

"Who first wanted to do the commercial in a Black church." Loretta started the car up again as the stickball play ended.

7

"Yo, lady!" A husky young man put his head near Loretta's. "Who that fine-lookin' mama you got riding with you?"

"Crystal Brown. Remember the name," Loretta said as they eased along, "she's going to be a star!"

"She already a star!"

Loretta glanced at Crystal and smiled. "We were on our way over here, and there was a fight on the avenue to our right." Loretta pointed without turning her head from the teeming street before her.

"Nostrand," Crystal said. "There's always a fight on Nostrand."

"Jim took a look and wanted to leave," Loretta said. "He's paranoid about Black people. Don't tell him I said so, but he is."

"Hey, I'm Black," Crystal said.

"Honey, you're so beautiful and fresh that he doesn't see you as Black. Also your eyes are a little Oriental. I think he sees you as more exotic than anything else," Loretta said.

"When we were shooting the fried chicken commercial, he told the photographer to stay away from you. You know, he wanted more ethnic types. But afterwards he came over to me and asked me to find out who you were."

Two young men in red jumpsuits crossed in front of the car when they reached Fulton Street. They looked from Loretta to Crystal and back again before going on their way.

"Mama has a headache," Crystal said. "I guess she told you."

"Nope." Loretta patted Crystal on the leg. "I told her."

"Come again?"

"You've been working with me for almost six months," Loretta said. "And your mother has been coming to every session. The problem with that is that it typecasts you as a child model. 'Mamas' always mean *children*. Pure and simple. I think it's okay for your mother to come along some of the time, but not when you're going to meet somebody like Jerry Goodwin."

"What's he like?"

"He's good," Loretta said. "He makes things happen. He can create. You take your average photographer—like the one we dealt with last week when you did the tank tops, remember him?"

"Right." Crystal remembered the two hours of posing she did for a newspaper layout.

"All right, that photographer took good clean shots. They'll be in focus, they'll be bright, and you'll look bright and good. But that's all. Jerry'll see other things."

"Like what?" They were stopped at a light.

"What you really are, sensational," Loretta said. "It's that simple. He'll look at you and say you're sensational, and he'll be able to do great things for you. You've got wonderful bones in your face and he'll see that. But he doesn't like any hassle. He's enough in demand that if he even *thinks* there might be a hassle, he'll walk away."

"Mama wouldn't hassle anybody," Crystal said.

"I know that, and you know it," Loretta said. "But Jerry doesn't know it. There are mothers who do nothing but hassle."

The ride across Brooklyn to Jerry Goodwin's studio was

like a tour to a different world for Crystal. From the all-Black section of Bedford-Stuyvesant to the mostly White area of Brooklyn Heights seemed more than the half hour it took Loretta to negotiate the distance.

The brownstone was unassuming in a row of other brownstones. The streets were a lot cleaner than they were in Crystal's neighborhood and the block less crowded.

"We're not being paid for today," Loretta said as they walked up the stairs. "Jerry wants to shoot some pictures with you and another girl. He's going on just what I've said. I haven't even let him see your portfolio, because I think it's too ordinary."

Loretta parked the car and they went to the basement entrance.

"Hi, Jerry." Loretta kissed the dark-haired man who opened the door. "I thought you gave up cigarettes."

"I can't give them up." Jerry Goodwin looked at the half-smoked cigarette in his hand, then ground it out in an ashtray. "I give up thinking about them, but I keep looking in my hands and there they are. It's all subconscious."

"Jerry, this is Crystal Brown." Loretta helped Crystal off with her coat. "Didn't I tell you she was sensational?"

"How old are you?" Jerry asked.

"Sixteen."

"Not bad." Jerry picked up a light meter and held it near Crystal's face. "One of your parents White?"

"Both of her parents are Black," Loretta said. "And very good-looking. Her father looks a little like a tan Smokey Robinson. You know who I'm talking about?"

"Loretta, I haven't lived in the Stone Age all of my life," Jerry said. "I do know about Smokey Robinson. I don't like the way he looks, but I know who he is."

"You put your own makeup on, honey?"

"Sometimes," Crystal said.

"Not usually," Loretta added.

"Just as well," Jerry said, nodding his head. "You want to take off your clothes so I can take a look at you?" he asked.

Crystal looked at Loretta.

"You have something she can put on, Jerry?" Loretta said. "Crystal's not comfortable nude."

"Look, Rowena's up in the studio," Jerry said.

"Rowena?" Crystal felt suddenly awkward, ill at ease.

"She was the girl Kendall used to launch the *I Dare* cosmetics," Loretta said. "She also did some work for Lanvin, didn't she?"

"Among other things," Jerry said. "I think she's yesterday's news, but I'm using her for some shots for the *Risa* account. Go up there and put one of the swimsuits on, and let's see what you look like."

"Jerry, she doesn't have a swimsuit body yet," Loretta said.

"She might for these shots," Jerry said. "Is that your real name, Crystal?"

Crystal answered that it was.

Crystal was surprised at how large Jerry's studio was. One side had two background rolls, one white and one black, suspended from the ceiling. On the other side there was a small jungle scene set up. She couldn't tell if the trees were real or not, but it looked real enough.

"Hello?"

Crystal jumped as the voice startled her. She turned to see a young girl standing in a doorway leading out of the studio. She was wearing a bathrobe.

"Hello," Crystal answered. "The photographer—Mr. Goodwin—told me to come up here."

"He gonna shoot you for *Risa*?"

"He just told me to put on a bathing suit," Crystal said.

"He's gonna shoot you for *Risa*," the girl said. "What are you, a five?"

"Yes."

"You Black or Chinese or something?"

"Black," Crystal said.

"You're really beautiful," the girl said. "What's your name?"

"Crystal Brown, and yours?"

"Rowena. I just use that one name. You work a lot? How old are you?"

"I've just been in modeling nine months," Crystal said. "All print work. And I'm sixteen."

"Try this suit," Rowena said, holding up a gold suit with black leopardlike markings. "It's really sharp. I used to be sixteen; I mean fresh and everything. You have a nice face."

"Thank you, so do you."

"Jerry's real good. He's the best. Some guys are real creepy and they don't make you look good, you know what I mean?"

"Yes," Crystal said, not really sure what Rowena meant.

12

"Is there a dressing room?"

"You can dress here," Rowena said. "Jerry wants me in this tiger-skin pattern, but I hate it because it makes my lines go the wrong way. You know what I mean?"

"I think so," Crystal said. She was undressing as quickly as she could to change into the swimsuit before Jerry Goodwin came into the studio.

"I've got a real nice body," Rowena said. "See?"

Crystal looked at Rowena, who stood with the bathrobe open. She was naked underneath, and she did have a nice body.

"You know how I got to be a model?" Rowena asked. "I was in the park with my kid brother, and Jerry came along and started taking pictures of me. I thought he was just trying to come on to me, you know what I mean? But he was kind of cute, so when he asked me my name and address I gave them to him."

"And he called you for a job?"

"Almost four months later," Rowena said. "A client came in and saw my picture on his wall. He said I was 'different,' and wanted to know if Jerry could get me. Jerry called up and was all cool and everything, but he really wanted me bad. He was flat-out broke. How'd you break in?"

"They were doing this commercial for fried chicken at my church," Crystal said. "They just shot the choir singing, and then cut to a family eating chicken at home. Anyway, this guy saw me and he mentioned me to Loretta, she's my agent."

"You take any classes or anything?" Rowena asked, stepping into the swimsuit.

"No. Loretta contacted me through the pastor of the church. She had a photographer she knows take some pictures to see how I looked. The pictures were okay and she started finding jobs for me."

"You've got a good face. You can probably look cool or hot or anything," Rowena said. "I've only got one look. You know, real sexy, like this . . ."

Rowena closed her eyes halfway and parted her lips slightly.

"Verrry sexy!" Crystal said.

"Yeah, that's cool," Rowena said. "But it's only one look. I can't look like a girl scout or anything like that. My eyes are wrong. I've got thick eyelids and that makes my eyes look too small. When I first started, I was really hot. Everyone liked my eyes, and then some other girls came along with my look. But I was still hot. Now I'm not so hot, but Jerry thinks my look will come back. I'm only eighteen, so I got time."

"I think you're pretty," Crystal said.

"I am," Rowena said. "But your look has to be in or you're dead. Jerry thinks I could go to Rome, where I'd be different and do a whole step number."

"Step number?"

"The fashion shows." Rowena smiled. She stepped backward three steps, then forward two steps and turned. "I did it once for a lady in Chicago. She kept giving me these steps to do, the kind they teach you in modeling school. You walk down this runway showing off the clothes. It's okay, but Chicago was so hot it was unbelievable. Maybe I can go back to doing that again."

"Jerry liked you," Crystal said, adjusting the strap that

came from the waist of the swimsuit. "Loretta, that's my agent, says he's really good."

"That's why I do anything he asks me," Rowena said. She seemed, for a moment, as if she were going to smile, and then she glanced quickly away. "I mean, just anything he asks me."

"Okay, girls, this is what I want." Jerry Goodwin finished adjusting the lights. "I want you to look sexy in these swimsuits. And sexy isn't wiggling your hips, Rowena. Sexy is what you feel and what you send out to the camera. I want you both to get into the set and crawl around like tigers— I guess it's tigresses."

Crystal watched as Rowena slipped out of the bathrobe and went on to the set. She thought Rowena looked great in the tiger-print suit. Rowena went down on her knees and started walking on all fours as if she were an animal.

"That's it!" Jerry said. "You got it, Rowena!"

The camera clicked and whirred as Jerry started taking pictures of Rowena. He had a camera on a tripod, which he looked down into. There was another camera on the wall, and he had a long cable release for that one.

"You want me to get in, too?" Crystal asked.

"Well, you're not here to paint the studio," Jerry said gruffly, without looking up.

Crystal got down on the floor of the set and started crawling around as she saw Rowena doing. Rowena was making noises, low noises, like an animal growling, and Crystal wondered if she had done this before.

"Get your rear end up, Crystal!" Jerry called. "Arch your back!"

She knew what Jerry meant, and how to do it. She had seen pictures of models doing that kind of thing, making themselves look as if their proportions were all wrong. Boys in school would look at magazines with the girls doing that and make comments. Crystal tried not to think about what she was doing so much. She imagined that she was an animal, slinking about in the jungle. The lights were hot, but not as hot as the photographer's lights when she modeled the tops.

"That's it." Jerry spoke as the cameras clicked. "Keep those backs arched."

Rowena was going crazy. Her face looked angry. She got down really low, so that her chest was on the ground and her rear end high. She started toward Crystal as if she were going to attack her, and Crystal backed away. Then Crystal moved toward Rowena, and Rowena moved back but not much.

"Look toward me and freeze, Crystal," Jerry said.

Crystal looked at him and smiled.

"Don't smile! Tigers don't smile!"

Crystal stopped smiling.

"Wake up, Rowena!"

Rowena put her hands on Crystal's back and then her head. It was hard for Crystal to imagine just what Rowena was doing. She tried to imagine what the pictures would be like, how they would look on the proof sheets. Images of herself crawling around in the small set combined with images of herself in church that morning.

"Okay, Crystal, come out of the set and let me get some shots of Rowena."

Crystal stood up and walked out of the set. She pulled the bathing suit down in front where it was binding into her thigh. There was a wooden chair by the wall, and she sat on it and watched as Jerry kept photographing Rowena. Rowena rolled and slid across the plastic grass of the set. She growled at the camera and used her hands as if they were claws to swing at it. Crystal wondered if Jerry really wanted Rowena to do that. She wondered what he really thought of her.

When the session was over, Jerry turned off the lights that were on the jungle set. Crystal watched him go from light to light, putting his hand in front of each bulb to see how warm it was after he had turned it off. He went back to the camera.

"Hold it!" Jerry held up his hand.

Crystal looked to where the camera was pointing and saw Rowena. She was in a robe and wiping the perspiration from her legs with the bathing suit she had been wearing.

Jerry didn't say much to Crystal afterward, just that he would be in touch with Loretta.

By the time Crystal got home, she was exhausted. There was a note on the refrigerator from her mother, saying that she was going to the store for milk and would be right back. Crystal took a shower and put on a robe. Her mother was home when she came out.

"How did it go?" Carol Brown leaned against the kitchen sink as she talked to her daughter.

"Okay," Crystal said. "Did Loretta tell you about the new foundation she wanted me to try?"

"I wanted to ask you about the session today." Crystal's mother had a cup of tea cradled in her hands. "I didn't tell your father that you were going to a photographer's studio by yourself."

"I don't think it was that big a deal," Crystal said.

"Then why did Loretta ask me not to come?"

"She said that some mothers are—you know—"

"I don't know," Mrs. Brown said. "Some mothers are what?"

"I guess they want to tell people what to do or something," Crystal said. "She also said that if your mother comes along, they think about you as if you're still a kid or something."

"And you're grown, right?" Carol Brown touched her daughter's hair to see if it was still wet.

"I didn't say that," Crystal said, returning her mother's smile.

"Girl, I was pretty when I was your age."

"You're pretty now, Mama," Crystal said. "Loretta said you could be a model. You could model for Sears. She even said it."

"That's behind me," her mother said. She had put on the water for more tea and now poured it into the dark porcelain pot. "What I did with my being pretty was go out and find a pretty Black man and think I had everything. I didn't even know how much was out there. I'm not going to stand in your way."

"It wasn't my idea, Mama," Crystal said.

"I didn't think it was," Mrs. Brown said. "I just wanted you to know that I'm pushing for you. And I don't think you should talk about going to the studio today with your father unless he brings it up."

"You going to tell him?"

"Nope. Crystal, let me tell you something about men. They all want to see pretty women, but they don't want their wives and daughters being seen," she said. "Believe it, child."

2

THE *CALIPER* WAS THE DUBOIS HIGH SCHOOL MAGAZINE. It had been once called *The Pen* but had been changed when another high school magazine of the same name won a prize in the regional contest. Crystal's homeroom teacher, Mrs. Sposato, said that not many students made it, but Crystal decided to try out for it anyway. She had submitted the required essay, filled out the questionnaire, and compiled a list of books she had read over the summer.

"Why do you want to be on the *Caliper*?" Mr. Dennison asked. He was the faculty adviser on the *Caliper*.

"I like to write," Crystal said. Mr. Dennison was nice looking. He had a strange way of turning his head to one side when he talked, but Crystal liked it. "I used to write poetry when I was in the seventh grade and my teacher said it wasn't bad."

"You write for any other school papers or magazines?" he asked.

"No," Crystal answered.

"So you've just been in magazines as a model?"

"You know about that?"

"I couldn't miss it," he said. "You're the biggest celebrity the school's ever had. Want me to tell you something? You're the first model I've ever talked to."

"This is the first magazine I've ever wanted to get on," she said.

"Okay, Miss Brown." Mr. Dennison smiled. "Let's you and I take a chance on each other. I think your experiences as a model might flesh out your writing a bit. Right now it's pretty thin. You put words together well, but there's not a lot of substance. I've scheduled a staff meeting in my office next Wednesday at three-thirty. If you have anything else you've written, I'd like to see it then."

He walked away, and Crystal wrote down the time of the meeting in the appointment book that Loretta had given her.

"Two things you have to be in this business," Loretta had said, "are beautiful and punctual."

"Crissie!" Crystal knew it was Pat. She was the only one she allowed to call her anything but Crystal.

"Hi, Pat, how's it going?"

"Terrible! There are two new boys, transfers." Pat carried her books in front of her. "One is cute and little, and the other one is cute and tall. So I take a look at both of them and they take a look at me because we're all in the library, see?"

"You taking that Library Science course?"

"It was either that or Gym, and I'm *not* taking Gym at nine o'clock in anybody's morning," Pat said. "Anyway, I de-

cided that I like both of them and I'm going to let th[...]
it out for me, see? Then they come over and they ask me [...]
of them I want to go out with first."

"They said that?"

"Yeah, child." Pat sucked her teeth. "Just as big as you
please."

"So what did you say?"

"I said I've got a steady boyfriend and I didn't go out
with boys my age, anyway."

"Since when did you get a steady boyfriend?" Crystal asked.

"I didn't, but I had to tell those fools something."

"You're too much, girl," Crystal said. "I just came from
seeing Mr. Dennison about the *Caliper*."

"You make it?"

"Yeah—he said he'd take 'a chance' on me."

"Is he married?"

"I don't know." Crystal caught a glimpse of herself in the
glass of the trophy case and pushed her hair away from her
face. "You think he's cute?"

"You talking about *the* Mr. Dennison? That gorgeous dude
who teaches English?"

"That's him."

"If I could write, I'd be there tomorrow trying out for the
Caliper," Pat said.

"How did the volleyball tryouts go?"

"I didn't make the team," Pat said. "They only had room
for two players, and they chose these two tall girls. That's
where I'm going now, to get my medical slip from Mr. Fishman. I think I'll try out for the lacrosse team."

"You play that, too?"

"I don't even know what lacrosse is," Pat said. "But I might as well try out for it."

There was a volleyball game going on in the gym, and they stopped to watch it for a while. Crystal saw the look on Pat's face as she watched the players. Mr. Fishman, the gym teacher, was also the volleyball coach. Pat asked him for her medical slip.

"You think I can make the lacrosse team?" she asked.

"I don't know," Mr. Fishman said. Then he turned to Crystal. "You play tennis or something, you seem familiar."

"Crystal's a model," Pat said. "She was in *Ebony* about a month ago."

"Washing my teeth," Crystal said.

"You trying out for any teams?"

"I don't think I'm athletic."

"Well, you certainly look healthy," Mr. Fishman said, smiling. Crystal smiled back.

The volleyball came bouncing in their direction and Crystal kicked it back toward the girls playing.

"That's not exactly how it's done," Mr. Fishman said.

"Why don't you teach Pat and she can teach me," Crystal said.

"Well . . ." Mr. Fishman looked at Pat. "Yeah, okay. I figure we can carry an extra girl on the team. Bring your things to the gym tomorrow after school."

"Did you hear that Jeannie wants to sing a solo next Sunday?" Crystal asked in the hallway outside of the gym. "John Williams told me."

"Who wants to sing a solo?"

"Jeannie," Crystal said. "Jeannie Curry."

"Oh."

"You think she shouldn't?"

"She can if she wants to," Pat said. "I mean, it's all right with me."

"Then why such a pitiful little 'Oh'?"

"If you knew how I busted my rear end trying to make that volleyball team—"

"He said you were on the team," Crystal said.

"Sure— I try like crazy for the team and he says no," Pat said, shaking her head. "You give him a smile and he says yes."

"Oh, you know how men are, Pat," Crystal said.

"Crissie Brown, this is your best friend talking, and you *know* I do not know how men are," Pat said. "However, I am willing to learn, and I'll take any help I can get."

"Did I tell you about the White model I worked with Sunday?" Crystal asked.

"What was she like?"

"You remember that model that was in the ads for *I Dare* perfume?"

"Uh-uh. I just started looking at models when you started doing it."

"Anyway, she was the one," Crystal said. "I took pictures with her Sunday."

"She rich?"

"She should be," Crystal said. "All the layouts she was in."

"Say, look, girl"—Pat stopped in front of the water cooler—"are you going to be rich?"

"How do you know I'm not rich now?" Crystal asked, giving Pat a nudge.

"Because I don't think you're stupid," Pat said. "You live on Gates Avenue, in the heart of the ghetto. Ain't nobody live there unless they are poor. If you are not poor, then you are stupid!"

"I'd like to be rich," Crystal said. "Who knows . . . maybe one day."

"Just don't forget your friends," Pat said. "You'll need me around to keep your books or something."

"If I get rich, we'll hire ourselves an English butler," Crystal said.

"What you mean?" Pat said. "We need two, and they can't be older than eighteen. And then we got to learn to walk around like we're fragile or something."

"Go on, girl." Crystal laughed as Pat sashayed down the hall to her next class.

Rich was something Crystal thought she could get used to being. At first she didn't think much about money. Modeling was just something she could do to help the family out. But that wasn't what Loretta was talking about.

"You don't get many chances to make real money in this life," Loretta had said. "When you see a chance, you have to reach out and snatch it. If you don't, somebody's going to, you can bet on that."

When she thought of having a lot of money, it was usually in some kind of silly way. She imagined a maid waking her in the morning with a silver bowl of cornflakes. Cornflakes with thin slices of fresh peaches with the fuzz cut off. Then the dream would switch to her mother. She would look so elegant being rich. She'd probably have a silver silk nightgown and a powder blue housecoat to wear over it. Her mother would like that. Her mother would know how to be rich, that was for sure. Her father, now that was another story.

When she got home, there were two phone calls on her message machine. One was from Loretta. She said that she had an offer from an agency dealing with a computer account.

"They want you to audition for a television spot." Loretta's voice coming from the answering machine seemed far away. "I think you're supposed to look adorable while your father explains how the computer works."

Crystal was excited when she called her agent but found that Loretta was against her taking the job.

"It sounds good to me," Crystal said.

"I don't think so," Loretta said. "I wanted to tell you about it, but I don't think we should make that kind of a move. If the agencies start seeing you around in that kind of spot, they want to keep you there. You can go from Bloomingdale's to Sears in this business, but you can't go from Sears to Bloomingdale's. At any rate, I think we should wait until we see what Jerry thinks about your pictures. Okay?"

"Okay."

"And don't forget we have a shooting tomorrow. I'll send a car for you in the morning," she said. "It's going to be there at four so get to bed e-a-r-l-y. They want to shoot between five-thirty and six. Got it?"

Crystal had said okay about the television but she hadn't

meant okay. She really wanted to try something on television. Sometimes Loretta was confusing. She would talk about needing to be exposed, and making it big, and then she would turn things down that Crystal thought would be just right for her.

The other call was from Pat. She wanted the History assignment.

"Don't do it," Crystal said. "Didn't you have to go for the tryouts during History?"

"Yeah, but I might as well do it," Pat said.

"Look, Pat," Crystal said. "If you're trying out for something in the school, then that's what you're doing. You're not going to History, and so you don't have to do your homework. I went to the *Caliper* and I'm not doing it."

"I guess you're right," Pat answered.

Crystal had thought about doing the History homework. She had promised her mother that she would keep up with her schoolwork. She didn't really *have to,* she knew, but she'd said she would. On the other hand, nobody expected her to be perfect.

Crystal had known Sister Gibbs for as long as she remembered. Her mother had said that she should stop doing Sister Gibbs' hair when she started working as a model. She couldn't, her mother had said, do everything that people from the church wanted her to, and they would just have to understand that. But the seventy-seven-year-old Sister Gibbs was special to Crystal. Crystal looked at the clock above the refrigerator and figured she could go upstairs and do Sister Gibbs' hair and still have time to get in her exercises before dinner. If not, she could always do the exercises after dinner.

"Crystal?" The small, thin woman leaned forward. "That you?"

"Yes, ma'am," Crystal replied.

"Well, if you're sure it's you, come on in." Sister Gibbs moved away from the door.

"I figured I could do your hair this afternoon instead of tonight," Crystal said. "If that's all right with you, of course."

"I don't know." Sister Gibbs sat at the kitchen table, her white hair just reaching the top of the high-back chair. "The little girl I used to know that did my hair used to do it in the evenings. Now this big glamorous woman come ringing my doorbell . . ."

"Sister Gibbs, now you just go on!" Crystal said.

"What you done heard in the streets that's juicy?" Sister Gibbs asked.

"Nothing much," Crystal answered. She had brought her combs and makeup kit with her and put them on the table next to the bowl of wax fruit that sat in the middle of a doily.

"What you mean 'nothing much'?" Sister Gibbs tilted her head back so she could look at Crystal through the bottoms of her bifocals. "When I was a young girl I could always find me something juicy to carry around. Now who out here doing the dirt?"

"Sister Gibbs." Crystal was behind the old Black woman, taking the bobby pins out of her hair. "You know the Bible says 'Judge not lest ye be judged.'"

"I ain't asking you to do no judging," Sister Gibbs said.

"I'm just asking you to do some reportin'! Now the Bible don't say nothin' about no reportin'!"

"Well . . ." Crystal loved working on Sister Gibbs' hair. It was so soft, it reminded her of spun silk. "I heard that Dotty, Sister Kaye's girl—you know who I'm talking about?"

"Skinny girl with a big butt," Sister Gibbs said drily. "Got about as much tittie as a boy."

"That's the one." Crystal smiled to herself. "I heard she was running around with Deacon Turner's cousin. I don't know if it's true or not, though."

"'Course it's true!" Sister Gibbs said. "They was over in that bar on Gates Avenue, 'cross from the funeral parlor, last Saturday night. Sister Williams told me she saw her coming out of it, and she walked up to her and asked her what she was doing in a bar when she was supposed to be at Bible study."

"What she say?" Crystal was gently brushing out Sister Gibbs' hair.

"Sister Williams said she come talking about how she was looking for her brother in there. Now you know Vernon don't be hanging out in no bars," Sister Gibbs said. "And Sister Williams said Dotty's eyes was as red as a fire truck. I know she been in there nippin'!"

"Her mother's really disappointed in her," Crystal said. "You want some henna in your hair?"

"What I want that mess in my hair for?" Sister Gibbs asked. "You go on and comb it out like you usually do and pin it up so it look nice. Maybe put some of that mousey in it. Now what you saying about her mama being disappointed?"

"I said I thought she would be disappointed if she knew she was in that bar," Crystal said.

"Humph!" Sister Gibbs turned to one side. "I don't see why she be so disappointed. I remember that hussy when she was wearing tight dresses down in Durham. You know anybody that come from Durham, North Carolina, and ask don't they know about them Greenes. That was what they was then, the Greenes.

"She and that no-good yellow brother of hers used to be the most notorious things down there. I didn't think she ever was going to get married. When she did, it was all of a sudden and we started counting. Sure as I'm sitting here, it wasn't but eight months to the day when she laid down and had that first kid of hers. And I'm telling you what the Lord loves and that's the truth!"

"I didn't think that Deacon Turner would want to have anything to do with her, though," Crystal said.

"Humph!" Sister Gibbs straightened up in the chair. "Them Turners ain't nothing but a bunch of Sunday School Christians. Butter wouldn't melt in their mouths if you see them on a Sunday morning. Got they Bibles under they arms and nodding at all the ladies. Especially that James with that gold tooth stuck up in the middle of his mouth like some kind of heathen! They all womanizers! Every one of them!"

"I ought to make you up real nice," Crystal said. "So when Brother Pugh comes around, he won't know what to say."

"Ain't no use in making me up, Crystal," Sister Gibbs said. "If that old man knew what to say, he wouldn't know what to do!"

"Sister Gibbs, I do believe you are getting fresh in your old age!" Crystal said.

"Don't you worry none about me being fresh, honey." Sister Gibbs looked in the mirror that Crystal put before her. "Me and the Lord got us a little deal. I done spent my life serving Him and now I can talk the way I want to. I knew how to live my life, though. You can't read the Bible and not know how to live your life."

"Yes, ma'am."

"You know how to live your life, Crystal," Sister Gibbs said. "I can tell that by the way you carry yourself. You just keep on living like you know you supposed to. Don't let nobody turn you around, girl."

"I surely won't."

"Let me see that mirror again."

Sister Gibbs looked at the mirror Crystal put in front of her.

"You look pretty good to me," Crystal said. "I still think I should make you up some."

"No, honey, that wouldn't do at all," Sister Gibbs said, shaking her head slowly. "How would it look? Me, a Christian woman, going around breaking these old men's hearts?"

Sister Gibbs laughed, and Crystal put both arms around the old woman's shoulders and hugged her. "Sister Gibbs, you are something else!" Crystal said.

"I know it." Sister Gibbs put her dark hands over Crystal's. "Now you get on home before your mama accuse me of stealing you!"

Crystal kissed her gently, got in a second hug, and left.

3

CRYSTAL HAD FINISHED A BREAKFAST OF TEA AND FRESH fruit by the time the limousine arrived. The driver, a thin, owlish man, was relieved when Crystal's mother said that he had the correct apartment.

"It's early, you know," he said, twisting his cap nervously in his hand. "You don't want to wake people up at this time of the morning and ask if they're expecting a limousine."

"Especially in this neighborhood." Daniel Brown was sitting in his robe at the table, a cup of black coffee cradled in his hands. "You want coffee?"

"No, sir." The driver glanced at the clock over the refrigerator. "We'd better start off; you can never tell how traffic is going to be."

"At *this* time of the morning?" Crystal's father asked.

The driver shrugged.

Crystal kissed her father good-bye. He grunted and shook his head. His lips tightened ever so much, and Crystal thought of the argument she had overheard when she came out of the shower. He didn't want her modeling without her mother's being there, he had said.

"Daniel, you can't take away the girl's chances," her mother had answered. "She has a chance to do something with her life. Are you going to take that, too?"

"What do you mean, *too*?" had come the angry reply.

"Nothing." The muted reply was scarcely audible through the bathroom door. So many of her parents' arguments finished with her mother ending the discussion by saying 'Nothing' to something her father had said.

"You be careful," her father said as she went out the door.

Crystal turned and smiled. "I will," she said.

The driver seemed to come alive once they had left the Black section of Brooklyn.

"Your mother's a looker, too," he said. "She ever a model?"

"No," Crystal said.

"How long you been modeling?" he asked.

"Not that long," Crystal said.

"You know who I had in the car about two weeks ago?" the driver asked, and then continued before Crystal could reply: "Michael Jackson's look-alike. The guy looked just like him."

"That's nice," Crystal said.

"I had that colored boxer in here once, too. What's his name—real dark guy—you know who I'm talking about."

"No," Crystal said.

"Yeah, anyway, I had him in here. He was okay."

The city in the early morning was eerie. The dark shadows of the buildings loomed ominously over the narrow streets. Crystal sat in the middle of the backseat as the car whisked into downtown Brooklyn and over the Manhattan Bridge. In Manhattan, there was already activity as trucks unloaded in Chinatown and the East Village.

She felt alone. It was more than the empty streets or being shut away in the speeding limousine. It was as if she were no longer herself but some other person being carried through the morning stillness to be something she was not. There was a picture somewhere, waiting for her presence. There were angles that she would fill, a glossy smile that she would place in just the right light, at just the right moment.

The early shooting was for an Italian magazine. Crystal didn't like working with foreign photographers that much, because sometimes she didn't understand their directions. When the limousine arrived at Fifth Avenue and Fifty-seventh Street, she felt nervous. The crew was already there. A young man came and opened the door for her quickly. She was glad to see Susan Hirsch, Loretta's secretary, on the sidewalk, close behind.

"Good morning, Crystal." The young man who had opened the door made a sweeping gesture with his hand. "I'm Frankie, and I'll be doing your makeup."

In a moment, Crystal was sitting in a small tent set up on the sidewalk outside of Tiffany's. The blouse she would be wearing hung on a padded hanger. Frankie looked at her face a long while and then put shadow on her cheeks.

"You have a marvelous face," he said, leaning close to her. "If you stay away from sugar, you'll never need anything except touch-ups for years. Maybe a little highlighter around the eyes. You should pluck your brows, though."

"They're not very heavy," Crystal said. Out of the corner of her eye she could see Susan sipping coffee.

"They don't have to be heavy," Frankie said. "You can always add in this business. It's the taking away that's hard. There. You're beautiful."

"Do you know the photographer?"

"He's not bad," Frankie said. "I don't think he's that good, either. He's a poser. He goes around striking poses and thinks he's wonderful. When they get tired of his photographs, his posing won't do a bit of good."

"He's hot. Anything he does they love," Susan said. "When you're hot, you don't have to be good."

The photographer ignored Crystal as the wardrobe lady and designer adjusted the blouse she would be wearing over the slim black pants. Crystal looked at herself in the mirror. She looked good.

"They're going to shoot you in front of the steel doors," Susan said. "Later, they're going to composite the perfume into the picture."

Frankie waited until all of Crystal's wardrobe was in place before putting the final touches on her hair. He brushed it up from the back and put a small circular comb in the center of the back, and then combed the hair out from it.

"It'll look fuller this way," he said.

"I feel like my scalp is being shrunk or something," Crystal said.

"Don't pay too much attention to what this guy says," Susan said. "He's very insulting. He's already called me a few names, and he's insulted everybody else, too. Just ignore everything except his directions."

"What's his name?"

"C-r-o-c-e," Frankie said, with an effeminate flourish of the hand. "It rhymes with okay."

The photographer's assistant took a light-reading, with

34

Crystal in front of the doors. Then the photographer came over.

For a while, Giovanni Croce just stood in front of Crystal, looking at her. Crystal stood looking back.

"Just try not to look too Black," he said, finally. Then he went back to his camera.

"Just look at the camera," the assistant called to Crystal.

Crystal stood, feeling angry from Croce's remark about her not looking "too Black" and awkward with the lack of direction, as the short, thinnish photographer shot several pictures. Then he turned away, and the assistant said that he had finished.

"I told you he was a pain in the rear end!" Susan Hirsch said. "He treats everyone like dirt, but he gets into all of the big magazines in Europe."

"Can you get the comb out of my hair?" Crystal asked.

Susan took the comb out.

"Hold it!" The assistant put his hand on Susan's shoulder and directed her away from Crystal.

"Just don't smile." Giovanni began to take more pictures of Crystal. He moved in front of her quickly, taking pictures from a lower angle than he had before.

Susan Hirsch looked behind Crystal and saw the sun breaking through the clouds over the distant buildings. In another moment, Giovanni had stopped and had merely walked away, leaving Crystal standing in the middle of the sidewalk.

Crystal saw that Giovanni had given his assistant his camera and had gone into his own limousine. She saw Susan speak to him and then come over to her.

"The guy's a real creep," Susan said. "I asked him how it went, and you know what he said?"

"I was too Black?" Crystal asked.

"He asked me why I would care!"

"It went strangely," Crystal said. The wardrobe people took the blouse, and Frankie brought her coat to her.

"You're very beautiful," the wardrobe lady said.

"Thank you," Crystal said.

"You were good," Frankie said. "He took extra pictures. He makes it such a big deal that his shots are so precious, but he took more pictures of you."

"Sure, she was good," Susan said. "You headed for school today?"

"Yes."

"The limo will take you later," Susan said. "Loretta wants to have breakfast with you. You eat anything yet?"

"Yes."

"So have coffee," Susan said. They took the limo to the Regency-Carleton, where Loretta lived, and called her apartment. They waited in the lobby for nearly ten minutes before she came down and then went to breakfast in the hotel's restaurant.

"How'd it go?" Loretta asked.

"Frankie said it went fine," Susan said. "Croce took some extra shots."

"He made me feel awkward," Crystal said. "I felt like a *thing*."

"That's what he wants," Loretta said. "A lot of people in this business are like that. They all have their reasons, but what they want most is for the girls to be anything but people. That way it's them that make the session work. You've got to be bigger than life to work your way through these people."

"How about just punching them out?" Susan said.

Loretta smiled and signaled the waiter. She ordered coffee for herself and Crystal, and Susan ordered eggs and toast.

"How did you like Jerry?" Loretta asked, after the waiter had left.

"He seemed okay," Crystal said.

"He was telling me that Joe Sidney is doing another picture. He wants to start principal photography next August."

"Joe Sidney's a director," Susan said. "He does a lot of pictures for the young market. Coming-of-age things, mostly."

"Garbage, mostly," Loretta said. "But he makes money for the studios. Anyway, he's got a big budget this time around and he's looking for a name male lead. I think he's making a big mistake—just because you make money with a cheapie doesn't mean you're going to make more money with a bigger investment—"

"That's right," Susan said. "Coppola didn't do too well with those Hinton things."

"And they were pretty good," Loretta said, nudging Crystal and pointing to two little old ladies at a corner table. "They're both richer than Midas and act as if they're dirt poor."

"They look nice," Crystal said.

"That's their act," Loretta said. "They're meaner than Gila monsters. Anyway, getting back to Joe Sidney . . . I don't think he can do anything for us, but I think we should be thinking about movies."

"I don't know anything about acting," Crystal said.

"Most of the youth things they're producing now are easy to act in," Loretta answered. "All you have to do is wear something that shows off your figure and act as if you checked your head at the door."

"A lot of this," Susan said. She put her hands under her chin and opened her eyes as wide as she could.

"That I can do," Crystal said, laughing. She imitated Susan just as the waiter came over.

"Ah, you are an actress, madame?" the waiter asked.

"Of course, she is," Loretta said, smiling. "Don't you see her talents?"

Susan's eggs were done so that they looked like white puffs of foam. Crystal saw Susan attack her breakfast as if she were really hungry while Loretta just played with her coffee.

"You think I could get a part?" Crystal asked.

"It's possible," Loretta said. "We could map out a campaign. Jerry had drinks with a secretary over at *La Femme* who promised to get him an interview with the publisher. Everybody shows up with pictures of good-looking girls, so he wants to show up with something different."

"Me?"

"Could be," Loretta said. "If the idea appeals to you, we can give it a try. Then, if you make *La Femme*, it'll be the kind of push we can use for the film people."

"Isn't *La Femme* sort of . . . ?" Crystal looked at Loretta. "Isn't that kind of a . . . you know . . . magazine?"

"You don't have to do it," Loretta said. "There are a lot of things you can do other than movies. It's just that with this business you have to make your mind up early. By the time something happens, a print special, a feature video spot hits, you need to have the next thing lined up."

"They're always looking for fresh people," Susan said. "But Loretta doesn't want to get involved with them on just any terms."

"I don't really think it's something that Crystal is interested in," Loretta said.

"I didn't say I wasn't interested," Crystal said, answering her agent's comment. "I'm interested; I just thought that *La Femme* was mostly nude."

"You wouldn't have to pose nude," Susan said.

"I wouldn't put you into anything like that," Loretta said. "You're going to have to make a decision, though."

"What's that?" Crystal asked.

"What you want for yourself," Loretta said. "And how badly you want it. I guess I have to know that, too."

"I think I'd like to get into pictures," Crystal said.

"Maybe we can talk about it next week," Loretta said, smiling. "Jerry wants to do a few more shots this Friday. You free?"

The limousine dropped Crystal off in front of the school, the driver coming around the back of the car to hold the door for her. Crystal nodded to the woman who sat near the front door. She was used to seeing Crystal come to school at odd hours and began writing a pass for her as she approached the desk. Crystal stopped in the third-floor bathroom to wash her makeup off before going to History.

"How was the French Revolution different from the American Revolution?" Mrs. Reyes was asking as Crystal walked into the room.

"Yo! Crystal, is that your limousine?" John Williams asked loudly enough for everyone to hear.

Crystal slid into her seat and put her books on her desk.

"I'd like to know, too," Mrs. Reyes said. "*Is* that your car? We saw it pull up to the school."

"No, my agent hires it for me," Crystal said.

"Get *bad*, mama!" John clapped his hands together.

"Okay, class, let's simmer down," Mrs. Reyes went on. "Crystal, did you do the homework?"

"I didn't have time, Mrs. Reyes. I had to go to the *Caliper* office."

"That's no excuse, Crystal," said Mrs. Reyes. "You can't let your modeling career interfere with your school assignments."

"I didn't say—"

"That's enough!" Mrs. Reyes' voice sharpened. "Did you do the reading, at least?"

"Yes," Crystal said sullenly.

"Good, then tell us the differences between the French and the American revolutions."

Crystal took a deep breath and exhaled slowly. Mrs. Reyes always got on her nerves. She glanced at the clock above the side blackboard. It was a quarter to ten, another ten minutes before the end of class.

"Crystal, do you intend to answer the question?"

"I don't know the answer," Crystal said.

"You'll see me after class," Mrs. Reyes said. "Frank, you want to give us one difference?"

"The people the French were fighting against, the kings and the royalty, they were right there," Frank said. "With the American Revolution, the king was across the ocean."

"That's one important difference," Mrs. Reyes said. "Pat?"

"The French people were more interested in getting more rights for the different classes while the Americans wanted to have a completely different country."

"Very good, Pat," Mrs. Reyes said. "Perhaps you should spend a little time with your friend Crystal convincing her that she's not royalty yet."

The rest of the class went quickly, and Mrs. Reyes was surrounded by students picking up test papers when Crystal walked out.

"Crissie, didn't Mrs. Reyes say she wanted to see you?" Pat caught up to her in the hallway.

"I thought you said you weren't going to do the homework?" Crystal said.

"I said maybe I wouldn't," Pat said. "But I had the time so . . ."

"So you figure you'd make me look like a fool!" Crystal said. "Thanks a lot."

"Have you seen my grades in History?" Pat asked. "Last year I had straight A's, and this year I'll be lucky to pull down a B."

"Look, Mrs. Reyes doesn't like me, and you know it," Crystal said. "She likes making me look stupid, and you're helping her."

"I think she likes you," Pat said. "Why would she have anything against you?"

41

"You heard that bit about the limo," Crystal said. "I think she's jealous, that's all."

"Just because you come to school once in a while in a limo?"

"And maybe because she's not very pretty," Crystal said. "Maybe she figures she'll show me up. How do I know?"

"People aren't like that, Crissie. I mean, just because somebody's not as pretty as you are, that doesn't mean they're out to mess over you."

"Then why *did* you do the homework?"

"Crissie!"

Crystal watched as Pat turned sharply and walked down the hallway from her. She and Pat had always been close friends, but there wasn't any question that Pat did a lot better than Crystal in school. What had the guidance counselor said? That Pat was definitely college material. Crystal had been maintaining a "C" average before she started modeling and was just barely managing that since she had been working.

It bothered Crystal to hurt Pat. They had been best friends for a long time, but the modeling seemed to get in the way somehow. There were times when she would be so glad to see Pat, to tell her what she had done during the day, and to talk things over with her. But more often than not she didn't talk to her about what was really on her mind, and sometimes she would find herself saying things that she knew had hurt her friend.

Pat had been as excited as Crystal when she found out that Crystal would be modeling. And Pat wasn't the jealous type, that wasn't it. It was just that modeling wasn't like she and Pat had thought it would be. The work was harder, more bor-

42

ing, than she ever thought it could be and made more demands on Crystal than she could handle at times. It was, Crystal felt, almost as if she were jealous of Pat for some reason. But she *was* pretty and she *was* making a lot of money doing what she was doing. There wasn't any need to apologize for that.

Still, Crystal wished that Pat could be with her some of the time. Maybe when she was waiting for a shoot to begin and heard the clients talking about her. Or when a job was done and everyone was packing up to go home, and no one seemed to care about anything except that the shoes she had been wearing looked good or that the name of the product was centered well in the pictures.

At breakfast the next morning, her father was putting too much butter on his toast, as usual, and talking up a blue streak, also as usual.

"So they want me to go to Chicago and show it to some bigwigs." Daniel Brown stirred just the top of his coffee as he spoke. "I don't know, though. Sometimes they get you in them big buildings and try to steal your ideas. They pick your brain and tell you they'll get back to you. Then the first thing you know they coming out with your idea and talking about how somebody else developed it."

"I don't see what's so wonderful about these dyes when you didn't even invent them." Carol Brown had poured a measured quarter cup of half-and-half into a mixing bowl with two eggs. "I think you're just frustrated because you're not a doctor."

"Frustrated?" Daniel's forehead furrowed. "Damn right,

43

I'm frustrated. Anytime you can't be what you want to be, you're either frustrated or a fool!"

"So what's your idea, Daddy?" Crystal was doing her face-stretching exercises in front of a makeup mirror on the table.

"Are you in pain or something?"

"Her facial exercises," Mrs. Brown said. "To keep her face firm. You wouldn't understand."

"You're right about that," Daniel said. "I sure don't understand what a sixteen-year-old girl needs to do exercises to keep her face looking good for. Suppose a ugly girl do the exercises, do she stay ugly?"

"Tell me about your idea, Daddy."

"Yeah, well, I figure if all the hospitals in the country would use these inert dyes to mark just what fluids should be administered only intravenously, then there would be a lot fewer accidents."

"If people were more careful, then there wouldn't be any accidents," Carol said.

"Yeah, but they ain't and that's that," Daniel responded. "Put some fire under the coffee, baby.

"Anyway, if I do go, I'll get a lot of recognition from the hospital," he went on. "Then, if they put my idea in practice, maybe they'll even name it after me."

"The Brown Plan?" Crystal looked up. "Sounds like Dull City to me."

"What's wrong with Brown? Brown's a nice name. If you were smart you'd look around for a boy named Brown to marry so you wouldn't have to change your name."

"Can't you think of anything else for your daughter

than getting married?" Crystal's mother asked.

"Loretta thinks I should just use Crystal. She says it has a nice feel about it."

"Sure does, baby." Daniel closed his eyes and put his head back. "I remember when I went to see you for the first time. I was working at Sydenham Hospital and you were born in Metropolitan."

"Do you want coffee?" Carol poured two eggs into a small frying pan and ran the whisk through them in a quick, counterclockwise motion.

"Yeah, give me a little more coffee," Daniel said, his eyes still closed. "The last snow of the season had just fallen and it was cold as anything for March. I was walking down along Fifth Avenue, and there was a newsstand with icicles hanging from it."

"I think I've heard this story a thousand times, and it doesn't get a bit better," Carol said.

"Yeah, it do," Daniel said. "Now listen to this part. I saw them icicles and they look just like crystals to me and that's how you got your name."

"If I had known that's what you were naming her after, I wouldn't have accepted it," Carol said.

"Crystal." Daniel opened his eyes and put his hand on his daughter's wrist. "The way your mama used to love me, I could have called you Snowflake and she would have loved the sound of me saying it."

"She still does, right, Mama?" Crystal was cutting the cantaloupe her mother had given her.

"Can you imagine?" Carol put the perfectly scrambled eggs

in the middle of the table. "If we had had a boy, he wanted to name him Roosevelt."

"After *Teddy*, not Franklin," Daniel said.

"What difference does it make?" Carol asked.

"It makes a lot of difference," Daniel said. "Franklin was a politician, Teddy was a fighter. That's what the Browns are, fighters."

"When you going to Chicago, Daddy?"

"They want me to go the end of October," Daniel Brown said. "I guess I'll go. What the heck, they can use the thrill of seeing a real Brown in action."

"Mama, did you tell Daddy?"

"I don't see why we have to discuss everything in the world with your father, Crystal," Carol said, glancing toward her husband. "We wouldn't, either, if he could drag himself out of the Stone Age."

"Tell me what?" Daniel Brown looked at Crystal.

"Daniel, please don't start acting colored," Carol said. She turned out the fire under the coffee and poured him a cup.

"Tell me what?"

"Loretta wants Crystal to go out with a boy in public so they'll be seen together."

"In public?" Daniel put two teaspoons of sugar in his coffee and stirred it. "Who's the boy, King Kong?"

"Sean Farrell, Daddy," Crystal said. "He was the teenager in 'America Incorporated' last year, but he's going to have his own show in the fall."

"This date is going to be in public?"

"Yes." Carol turned and looked at her husband. "They'll be

taken to a nightclub in a limousine, stay for two hours, and then Crystal will be brought back to the house in the limousine."

"Yeah, so why you so worried about me acting 'colored'?" Daniel asked.

"Sean Farrell's White," Crystal said.

"You are the funniest people in the world," Daniel Brown said, shaking his head. "You keep thinking I got something against White folks and I don't. I mean as long as this whole thing is in public, it's okay. You just take a hatpin or something along in case he gets frisky in the back of the car."

"I heard he wasn't the frisky type," Crystal said, smiling.

"You can't tell about them show-business types," Daniel answered. He brought the coffee to his lips and tasted it. Then he made a face. "This is the worse coffee I have ever tasted in my whole life, woman. Didn't your mama teach you nothing?"

"Not enough," Carol Brown said.

"Now what's that supposed to mean?" Daniel asked. "Crystal, what is your mother talking about?"

Crystal shrugged and stretched her face in the mirror, this time sticking out her tongue. Her father did the same thing and they both laughed.

4

LORETTA SAID THAT SHE WOULD BE WORKING ALL DAY for Crystal, and that Crystal, in turn, would be working for two hours for her.

"Jerry called this morning—he has this shoot to do with the Waterman agency, something about Swiss watches. He was going to let it go by, but then he thought about shooting you and Alyce Winslow together."

"Who's Alyce Winslow?" Crystal was in the back of the limo with Loretta, facing her on one of the small seats.

"She was with Mannequin, but now she's with Corolla. She's *very* hot. I understand she's not very nice, though."

Crystal shrugged.

"When Jerry asked if you were free this morning, he was really beside himself. He apologized all over the place, but I think we have to bend for somebody like Jerry once in a while—don't you think so?"

"I don't mind," Crystal said. "It beats Geometry."

"I even picked up the wardrobe for him," she said, indicating the boxes on the seat next to Crystal. "We still have to do the thing with Sean Farrell tonight, too. Do you know Rosemarie's column in the *Journal*?"

"I've seen it," Crystal said. "It has all the inside information on stars and everything."

"You're going to be in it tomorrow," Loretta said. "Rosemarie owes us. You'll change at the office."

"Okay," Crystal said. "Do I go back there after I leave the club?"

"No, I don't think so." Loretta leaned across and looked closely at Crystal. "Do you have a base on?"

"No."

"You're marvelous," she said. "I'd kill to have skin like yours."

"Black?" Crystal asked.

"Maybe not Black—no, wait—if I got the youth to go with it, I'd take the Black, too," Loretta said.

"You're so sweet," Crystal said.

"Only because you're so lovely," Loretta said. "And speaking of lovely, have you ever seen Sean Farrell? He's beautiful! And he's going to try to outshine you tonight. But we have a little something special planned. It was Rosemarie's idea. We might even get the top of her column."

"Will I see you later?" Crystal asked as they pulled up outside of Jerry Goodwin's studio.

"No, I have to go and talk to the movie people about you. I want to talk to them today, and then tomorrow they'll see the column, et cetera. It builds."

"I feel like a project," Crystal said.

"You are, baby," Loretta said as they stood in front of Jerry's brownstone. "You're getting seven-fifty for the shoot this morning. I sent your mother a check last week, did she get it?"

"Yes," Crystal answered.

"How are you doing for money?"

"Fine," Crystal said. "I've never had so much money in my life. I've never even dreamed of so much."

"Think about this, baby," Loretta said softly and slowly. "Modeling is a tough racket. You have to put up with a lot of garbage. You're *earning* this money. No one is giving it to you. Watch for Rosemarie's leads tonight."

Jerry had a problem with the lights flickering and was trying to find the landlord. He told Crystal to go up to the studio.

"Alyce Winslow is there already," he said. "Rowena's there, too. She'll fill you in on the details."

Going up the stairs to the studio the second time was different from the first. Crystal felt more comfortable with it than she had the first time, and she was glad to see Rowena again. She rarely had time to talk to other models. Even when there were other girls on the same job, they rarely spoke. The mothers of the other girls would be fixing their hair or somehow fussing with them or just talking to them while they stared at each other, especially during auditions.

There was usually a lot of staring. Crystal would stare at the other girls to see how attractive they were, or if their bosoms were more developed than hers. They would look at one another's hair or legs or the way each girl moved, and compare themselves. It was not one of the nicer parts of the job.

A tall, incredibly thin man brushed past Crystal as she went into the studio. He seemed annoyed. Crystal turned to watch him storm down the stairs she had just climbed and into Jerry's first-floor apartment.

"Oh, are you Crystal?" The voice from behind her had a slight English accent.

"Yes." Crystal turned to see a young girl, near her own age, sitting astride a chair.

"I'm Alyce Winslow," the girl said. "That mad, mad stork was my tutor. He's quite annoyed that I don't choose to learn anything about subjunctive clauses."

She was the most exquisitely beautiful girl that Crystal had ever seen. The brown hair, disappearing behind her shoulders, framed a face that Crystal somehow remembered from storybooks. She was the beautiful princess of every story that Crystal had ever read. Her eyes were blue but not the sparkling kind that Crystal had seen in some White models. Instead, they were incredibly calm and distant.

"I'm glad to be working this morning," Crystal said. "I would have Geometry if I didn't."

"Do you go to school?" Alyce asked.

"You could call it a school," Crystal said. "I'd call it a zoo."

"Jerry told me you were beautiful, but I couldn't imagine how you would look," Alyce said. "I like to do that, to hear about someone and imagine how they might look."

"How did you think I would look?" Crystal asked.

"Well, of course he said that you were Black, so I imagined someone darker," Alyce said. "I thought of Iman, the African girl. I envy her neck. Then I thought you might look like one of the rock stars. But you're quite special. You're vulnerable."

"Vulnerable?"

"It means that you look as if you can be hurt easily," Alyce said. "Men like that sort of thing, I'm told."

"I think you're very attractive," Crystal said.

"But I'm different than you, so we won't be competing," Alyce said. "We'll work well together. I have a cold look. Men adore that in young girls."

"Do you know what we're doing today?"

"Probably nothing. The electricity's not right or something and Jerry think's he's too upset to work. He's already spoken to the account, and they've agreed to put off the shoot until next week."

"Oh, he didn't tell me that," Crystal said.

"He's upset," Alyce said. "Have you seen Rowena?"

"No. Jerry said she's here, though." Crystal slid down the wall until she reached the floor.

"She's slinking around in Jerry's bathrobe." Alyce smiled with her mouth, but her eyes didn't change expression. "I'm supposed to work with her next Wednesday, but I don't have to if I don't want to."

"For Jerry?"

"No, for Bob Stiller. Do you know him?"

"I don't think so," Crystal said.

"He's fat and all hands, if you know what I mean. Rowena probably likes him."

"Here she comes," Crystal said, noticing Rowena bringing in a bowl of fruit.

"Hello, Rowena." Alyce put her head to one side and smiled. This time her whole face lit up. Crystal wondered if her smile was as good as Alyce's.

"Hi, Jerry said it looks like it's really off," Rowena said. "I mean, the stupid electricity! That kind of stuff really bugs me."

"I was telling Crystal that I was looking for someone to work with when I shoot with Bob Stiller next Wednesday," Alyce said. "I have to figure out who's free."

"I'm working with you," Rowena said. "Jerry said it'll be good for me to work in jewelry again."

"The guy from the account said I could choose," Alyce said matter-of-factly, as she rose from the chair, turned it around, and sat again. "I told him I didn't like working with just anyone."

"Oh?" Rowena looked at Alyce.

"The account doesn't use Blacks, so that leaves Crystal out," Alyce said. "Who do you think I should choose, Rowena?"

"Do you want fruit?" Rowena asked, holding out the bowl.

"Any bananas?" Crystal asked.

Rowena took a banana from the bowl and handed it to Crystal.

"Are you free Wednesday?" Alyce asked, turning to Crystal. "Maybe I could get the account to change his mind."

"I—I don't know," Crystal said.

"Are you free, Rowena?" Alyce asked.

"You know I am," Rowena said. "We were supposed to do the shoot together."

"I could work with you; it might be nice," Alyce said. "I would, too, if you would do me a favor. Would you?"

"What kind of favor?" Rowena asked. She sat cross-legged

on the floor, answering without looking at the younger girl.

"Well, you see"—Alyce crossed her legs and looked over to where Crystal watched in fascination—"I was told that to be a really great model you had to experience all sorts of things that great women experienced. And I imagined that I was a queen of a faraway place. . . ."

"I do that sometimes," Rowena said, looking up. She was eating an apple, and the juice from it moistened her full lips. "Once I imagined I was a princess and—who was it?—oh, yes, Mel Gibson rescued me from the Huns or some other sort of bad guys. I was a princess and my mom was the queen. It was a neat dream."

"I imagined I was a queen and my subjects came and asked me for bread," Alyce said. "And, being a good queen, of course, I gave it to them. And then each of them curtsied to me three times in gratitude. I thought, in the dream, that it was a nice feeling. That if I could do it in real life, it could be useful if I ever got a job that needed that sort of feeling."

"You want a job as a queen? You're too young," Rowena said. "You'd have to be a princess."

"Rowena, if you do me a favor and curtsy to me three times, so I would know how it felt, I will do you a favor and work with you next Wednesday."

Rowena didn't move.

The windows of Jerry's studio were covered with white sheeting. The morning sun, slanting through them, caught the dust in the air and made it shimmer. The soft light was becoming to Alyce as she sat, head high, almost motionless, in the chair.

Crystal pushed the peels of the banana together and held them as if the banana were again whole. Then, one by one, she let the peels fall, revealing the half-eaten flesh within.

"Rowena?" Alyce's voice broke the stillness.

Rowena didn't move.

Crystal, from the corner of her eye, saw Alyce's head move. Crystal looked up to see Alyce looking at her and smiling. Then the girl turned away and spoke again.

"Rowena?"

Rowena got up and stood before Alyce. Crystal held her breath as Rowena curtsied slowly once, twice, and then a third time. Then Rowena turned quickly and picked up the fruit bowl.

"Want any more fruit?" she asked, smiling.

"No," Crystal answered, not looking at her.

"Better save it for Wednesday," Alyce said. "You know how long Bob takes in his shoots."

Rowena took the fruit and left.

"Do you think that was cruel?" Alyce asked after Rowena had left.

"I don't know," Crystal said. "I mean, if it was really a dream . . ."

"I think it was," Alyce said, smiling prettily.

"Darling"—George looked over Crystal's head at her mirror image—"it's not going to be easy to do you."

"*Do* me?" Crystal wrinkled up her nose.

"Don't wrinkle your nose, it'll only lead to permanent wrinkles later on."

"Okay." Crystal forced a smile. She didn't particularly like George. He always made her feel uncomfortable somehow, in a way that most older men didn't.

George was in his late forties, perhaps even early fifties, Crystal couldn't tell. He was a striking-looking man with silver-gray hair and sharp features. What made him look odd to Crystal, at least close up, was the fact that he always wore a powder base and eyeliner.

Crystal sat stiffly in front of the makeup table as George fluttered about her, carefully applying her makeup. First there was the liquid foundation that was slightly lighter than her skin color.

"You have good skin and it'll last as long as you take care of it." George put different-colored face powders on the inside of Crystal's arms. "You'll have trouble if you ever try to get a face-lift, though. You people scar easily."

"I'm only sixteen," Crystal said.

"It won't last, believe me," George said. He selected the powder he preferred and sponged the others off.

"That's a different powder than I've been using," Crystal said.

"Fashion Fair is very good," George countered. "And it's different than you've been using because Loretta wants you to be different than you've been."

"How?"

"Keep still," George said as he applied the translucent powder. "You're going to be in your twenties tonight."

Crystal watched in the mirror as George worked. He dusted her face very gently and then began applying highlights. He worked slowly, stepping away from her now and again to see how he was doing.

"Don't sweat," George said as he wielded the small sponge he used. He highlighted Crystal's cheekbones, blending the light powder carefully upward toward her temples, making her eyes appear slanted. It was a nice effect, making her look almost Asian.

"How can I keep from sweating?" Crystal said, without moving her face.

"Think about money," George replied. "Money thoughts are very calming when you have the stuff."

"How do you know I have money?" Crystal asked.

"Stop talking," George said. "You have youth and you look delicious. It's like having a blank check. You just have to decide how many signatures you'll take. Lift your chin up."

Crystal lifted her chin.

George did Crystal's eyes with dark-brown eye shadow, making them look deeper, adding years to her face. There were touches of highlighter on her brows and deep gold on the lid itself.

The last bits of roundness from her face were taken out with contour shadow on her cheeks. Crystal hardly recognized herself in the mirror.

"Don't be surprised," George murmured. "Given a decent bone structure, and enough time, I can perform all sorts of little miracles."

"I do look older," Crystal said.

"Ssh!" George put on the lipliner and brushed on two shades of lipstick, a brown shade on her upper lip and a reddish-brown shade on her lower. Then he touched them lightly with gloss.

"You have wonderful lips," he said.

"Thank you," Crystal said. She stared at herself in the mirror. "Did Loretta—"

"Yes." George answered Crystal's question before she asked it. "Loretta asked me to make you up to look like a kumquat that's just right for the harvesting."

"What does that mean?"

"It means that she believes in you, I guess," George said. "And Crystal, *do* put your dress on carefully; it's rather flimsy."

The dress was an iridescent white wraparound with a toga-style neck. When the draped material was fastened by two small catches at the hip and waist, a slit exposed her left leg from mid-thigh. The hem was higher on the left, cutting from just above the left knee to just below the right. It was stunning.

"What do you think?" Crystal asked.

"If I were the type to be excited about such things," George said, "I would be."

"Do you mean that?" Crystal asked.

"Yes, I do."

He produced white feather earrings, which he put on her.

"*Hmmm*, nice." Crystal turned her head to see the earrings in the mirror.

"I see you're getting in the mood for the evening's festivities," George said. "I think I have something else for you, too. Loretta didn't say to have you wear this, but you simply must."

George left the dressing room. Crystal looked at herself in the mirror again. She smiled as she realized that she couldn't *not* look at herself. In the back of her mind, she had thought about George standing in the room as she took off her school clothes. He didn't really count, she thought.

"Here, let me try this on you," George said, returning.

It was an ermine stole, which George threw casually around Crystal's shoulders. The silk lining was cool against her bare skin and, when she turned her cheek, the fur was whisper-soft against her cheek.

"Now, say 'I am dee-vine,'" George said. "And mean it."

Crystal smiled, her even white teeth just barely visible between her full lips. "I am dee-vine!" she said. And she meant it.

"Here, turn and take a good last look," George said. "You can't stare at yourself in public, you know."

Crystal looked as George turned her gently by the shoulders.

Crystal Brown, she said to herself, you *are* divine.

The limousine was to take her to Fifty-seventh and Fifth, where she was to meet Sean Farrell at the Palm Court in the Plaza. The driver chatted amicably as they wound their way through the late-evening Manhattan traffic.

When the chauffeur opened the door of the limo in front of the Plaza Hotel and Crystal stepped out, she felt that all eyes were on her. A middle-aged man turned away from the woman he was with to look at Crystal and she saw the woman turn the other way as she passed them and made her way slowly up the stairs of the fashionable hotel.

She had been to the Palm Court before with Loretta for lunch. She walked slowly across the entrance lobby, aware that people were looking at her, probably wondering who she was.

"Crystal?" A short, heavyset man had crossed over to her and stopped her in front of the entrance to the Palm Court.

"Yes?"

"I'm Richard Sugarman, Sean's manager," the man said. "Loretta probably mentioned my name."

"Yes," Crystal said, not remembering the man's name at all.

"Yeah, well, Sean was supposed to meet you for a drink in the Palm Court, but he really doesn't want a drink so he figured the two of you could go straight over to the club, okay?"

"Oh, all right," Crystal said. "Where is Sean?"

"He's up in his room now," Sugarman said. He looked Crystal up and down. "You're really a good-looking girl."

"Thank you." Crystal smiled.

"Loretta said you were, but . . ." Sugarman shook his head. "Look, I'll give Sean a call. Why don't you have a seat?"

Crystal looked at her watch. It was eight-thirty; they had plenty of time. They weren't supposed to be at the club until nine. She watched as Sugarman used the house phone. He spent three or four minutes on the phone, turning several times to look at her.

"He'll be right down," Sugarman said after he had hung up the phone and come over to where Crystal was sitting. He pulled a chair closer.

"We have time," Crystal said.

"Yeah, sure." Sugarman wiped the side of his face with his fingertips as he spoke. "How long you in this business?"

"A few months," Crystal answered.

"Yeah, well, nothing wrong with that," Sugarman said.

"Sean's been in show business for a long time?"

"Yeah, you could say he was born in the business. His father did commercials and his mother was in about seven movies in this country, and she did the voices in two of them Godzilla movies."

"Oh, maybe I've seen her."

"Yeah, yeah, could be." Sugarman's hand went to his face again. "You know, you don't look Black. I don't mean there's anything wrong with that . . . But it's probably easier if you don't look too ethnic. You could be Chinesey or Hawaiian or African—something like that."

"I guess."

"Sean, he don't like these arranged things, but it's part of the business, you know."

"That's what Loretta said."

"Where do you live, the West Side?"

"Brooklyn."

"I bet a nice-looking girl like you has lots of boyfriends," Sugarman said.

Crystal looked away.

"I didn't mean to offend you," Sugarman said.

"I guess to some people it comes naturally," Crystal said.

"Yeah."

It was another fifteen minutes before Sean Farrell came down from his room and walked toward the front of the Plaza.

"Oh, look, there's Sean now." Sugarman jumped to his feet. "The car's outside."

Sean Farrell was shorter than Crystal had imagined him to be, but Loretta was right, he was beautiful. His eyes were a deep blue, almost sparkling. He wore a tuxedo that fitted him well. It was formal but, at the same time, he looked very comfortable in it.

"Well, I'm Crystal."

Sean didn't answer. He looked from her to Sugarman. "Did you tell her what side I wanted her on?" he said.

"No, er, look"—Sugarman shifted his weight from one foot to the other—"Crystal, we want you on Sean's left side. Now, if you forget, he'll just move you to that side. Now, if they're taking pictures of the two of you, he'll be on your right and they'll take pictures from the right side. Now, I don't want pictures of you two together."

"What? I thought that was the idea—"

Sean turned away.

"I mean you'll be together but not touching. There should be a few inches between the two of you. That way any pictures come out good for both of you. You know what I mean?"

"I know what you mean," Crystal said. She remembered Loretta saying that Sean would try to outshine her. She had expected something a bit more subtle.

"Try to keep this in mind, now," Sugarman continued. "There'll be no standing-still pictures. If the two of you are standing still and you see a photographer coming toward you, just walk away. Or Sean'll walk away from you."

Crystal glanced at Sean, who was staring out the door. She wondered if he was wearing shoes with high heels. She glanced down as Sugarman went on.

"And Crystal, don't touch his face. He really doesn't like his face being touched. So don't put your hands on his face, and don't, you know, kiss him. If you want to touch him, you can touch him on the arm or on the hand. I don't mean holding his hand, just touching it."

"He doesn't want to be touched," Crystal said. She noted that Sean wore elevator shoes.

"I'm sure it's going to be a wonderful evening for both of you," Sugarman said. "Here's the limousine now."

Crystal turned as Sean started for the car.

"Is he angry at something?" Crystal asked.

"Sweetheart." Sugarman grinned. "You're trying to make it, he's already a star. He's not here to entertain you. Let's leave it at that, okay?"

Sean waited at the car. Crystal forced a smile as she passed Sean and settled herself on one side of the large, upholstered seat. Sean entered quickly behind her and in a moment the door was closed.

"Whose idea was it?" Sean said, looking straight ahead of him despite the presence of Sugarman's large head in the car window. "To get a white limousine?"

"It's what they sent over." Sugarman's eyebrows raised together. "It don't make no difference."

"I guess it just *happened* to match her dress?" Sean said.

"You want her to change it?" Sugarman asked.

"I'm not changing *anything*," Crystal said through her teeth.

"Let's go, let's go." Sean waved his hand impatiently.

Sharo's was one of the finest clubs in New York. It usually featured a well-known pianist who played a combination of old standards and new tunes in a way that seemed to blend with the endless tinkling of glasses and chatter that filled the main room. It was decorated in the style of the Gay Nineties, complete with brass ornaments and waiters with long sideburns. The club had become the "in" place to be seen in and to see the rich and the famous.

Sean had not spoken to Crystal during the ride to the club. They had been expected, Loretta had taken care of that; a few minutes after they were seated, a waiter brought them drinks without taking an order. Crystal was surprised. Her drink came in a tall glass with a slice of pineapple attached to one side. It tasted like a milk shake.

"You're not exactly the friendly type, are you?" Crystal said. "I don't know why you even bothered to come."

"I don't think I need to be seen with some girl who hasn't done a darn thing in this business or any other business," Sean said. He sounded angry but his face never changed expression. Crystal liked that.

"So why are you here?"

"My agent thinks I need this kind of exposure. It's time I got away from immature parts."

"Oh." Crystal looked away from Sean and tapped her fingers nervously on the table.

"You're supposed to be looking at *me*," Sean whispered.

Crystal turned and Sean was looking right at her. He seemed taller when he was seated than he did standing. Crystal knew why he wanted to be photographed sitting. He had a long body but short legs.

"What would you like to talk about?" Crystal said. "I can't just sit here and *look* at you!"

"Why don't you tell me what you're doing now?" Sean said. "Sugarman tells me you're being considered for some part in a movie?"

"Loretta's mentioned something about movies, but nothing definite."

"You're better off," Sean said. "When they say things are definite in the movie business, what they really mean is that there's an outside chance."

"You want to dance?" Crystal asked.

"Are you kidding?"

The piano player had left and a small group was playing a schmaltzy Lionel Ritchie tune. It was a lovely place. Crystal was enjoying it, even though she wasn't enjoying being with Sean.

"I like this place," she said.

"Ever been to anyplace like it?"

"No."

"You'll get used to it," Sean said. "It's all part of the life. You have to learn to enjoy it without letting it get to you. I don't see how you can go that far. Most Blacks don't really make it big."

"Thanks a lot!" Crystal turned away from Sean.

A curl of blue smoke went up from another table, found its way through a shaft of light from one of the small overhead spots, and up into the darkness of the ceiling. Crystal imagined herself singing in the club, leaning against the piano.

"Well, who do we have here?" A husky female voice interrupted Crystal's thoughts. "Why, it looks like Mr. Sean Farrell—and a friend."

Rosemarie Montag stood in front of their table with a drink in one hand and a long cigarette holder in the other.

"Well, New York's favorite columnist." Sean raised his glass to her. He looked, to Crystal, very mature.

"Do I smell an *item* for my column here in the murky shadows of Sharo's?" Rosemarie asked, leaning toward the table.

"I couldn't stand to be in that wicked column of yours, Rosemarie," Sean said.

"And who is your lovely friend?"

"This is Crystal," Sean said. He gently put his hand on Crystal's. "She's a rather special friend."

"Oohh." Rosemarie sipped her drink and looked at Crystal as if she were completely surprised to meet her. "How marvelous! Hello, Crystal."

"Hello," Crystal replied softly.

"You are a lovely young thing," Rosemarie said, slurring her words slightly. "Sean is very lucky."

"There's nothing . . . official," Sean said, relaxed.

To Crystal, Sean looked exactly the way he had on "Love Boat."

"I'll keep your 'nonofficial' status in mind," Rosemarie said.

"I'm really trying to relax before the series begins. . . ," Sean said. "We have to start shooting in—"

"Oh, isn't that . . . ?" Rosemarie waved at someone passing by. It was Earl Morgan, the actor the movie magazines had labeled "the Black Clark Gable."

"Earl!" Rosemarie waved him over.

Earl Morgan threaded his way through a crowd of well-wishers, flashing the smile and the dimples that had made his reputation on the screen. He kissed Rosemarie lightly on the cheek.

"Oh, I'm going to faint, you handsome brute!" Rosemarie put the back of her hand against her forehead.

"Hello, lady," Earl's husky voice crooned.

"Earl, why is it that all the handsome men only kiss me in public?" Rosemarie said with a smile.

"If you'd leave a trail of crumbs, I'd gladly follow you to some private place," Earl said.

"Crumbs? I'd leave loaves of French bread if I was sure you'd be picking them up." Rosemarie sipped her drink and then looked toward Sean again. "Earl, you have to meet my old friend, Sean. You've seen him a thousand times on the tube. His star is very high and still rising."

"Pleased to meet you, my man." Earl extended his hand.

"My pleasure," Sean said, shaking the extended hand.

"And this is his friend—what did you say your name was, honey?" Rosemarie asked.

"Crystal."

"Well"—Earl took Crystal's hand in his—"any new friend of Rosemarie's is a new friend of mine, too. May I have this dance?"

The band was playing an upbeat tune. Crystal couldn't believe she was actually dancing with Earl Morgan. There were photographers all around them, and Crystal was only vaguely aware that they were taking pictures.

Earl talked to Crystal as they danced, asking if she was from New York and had she ever been to Hollywood. Crystal wasn't sure what she was saying in return. Earl's voice was like a cat's purr in her ear. He danced well, and she wondered if he could feel her heart beating against his chest.

When the dance was over Earl Morgan took her hands in his and held them so the fingertips came together. And then, as he looked into her eyes, he kissed her fingertips and thanked her for dancing with him.

When Crystal sat down next to Sean Farrell, he seemed annoyed.

"I hope that Morgan's not trying to cut me," he said. "You know that part that Eddie Murphy played in *Beverly Hills Cop* was originally supposed to be for a White guy."

"You think he's trying to cut you?" Crystal asked.

Another columnist, one that Crystal recognized, came over.

"Hi, I'm Jim Carroll," he said. "Wasn't that Earl Morgan you were dancing with?"

"Yes," Crystal said. "It was."

"And you're . . . ?"

"Crystal."

"Just Crystal?"

"Yes."

"Hi, Sean, how's it going?" Carroll turned to Sean.

"Not bad," Sean said. "Got the series coming up and I'm

considering a part in a Costa-Gavras flick, so things can't be too shabby."

"You and Costa-Gavras?" Carroll looked at Sean and shrugged. "Could be, I guess, could be."

The rest of the evening Crystal spent looking into Sean's eyes and thinking about Earl Morgan. People kept coming by their table and speaking to Sean, most of them asking who Crystal was. When Sean said that the evening was a success and it was time to go, she followed numbly to the waiting limousine.

When Crystal got home, it was almost three in the morning. Her father was in his shirtsleeves in front of the house drinking a beer. The wooden box he was sitting on leaned at a precarious angle to the red-brick wall.

"Hi, Daddy," Crystal said.

"Don't 'Hi, Daddy' me, girl." Daniel Brown turned his head away. "You know what time it is?"

"The limo brought me home."

"The hell do I care about that?" Angry lines appeared on his forehead. His eyes were bloodshot and the smell of stale beer on his breath made Crystal nervous.

"I'm sorry, Daddy." Crystal put her hands on her father's. "I didn't think I was going to be out this late."

"You have a good time being out here all hours of the damn night?"

"It was okay."

"What you mean it was *okay*?"

"It was really kind of great," Crystal said.

"You gonna tell me all about it, so I can eat my heart out?"

"Yep, even the part about me dancing with Earl Morgan!"

"Earl Morgan? Get out of here!"

"Really!"

"Well, let's get on upstairs. You can tell me about it in the morning. I'm too mad to listen tonight."

"I'm sorry, Daddy."

"Ain't no child looking as good as you supposed to be out this late, girl."

"You really think I look good tonight, Daddy?"

"Crystal"—Daniel Brown turned and took his daughter's face in his hands—"sometimes I look at you and see how good you look and it scares me. Being as pretty as you are and all, it may make you think it's all too easy."

"It seemed pretty easy tonight, Daddy."

"Yeah, honey." Daniel Brown and his daughter, Crystal, their arms around each other, started up the stairs. "But I still got to find out if Earl Morgan got frisky. I mean, if he did I'm going to have to go knock him out."

"He said he was going back to Hollywood tomorrow."

"That's okay, baby, people get knocked out in Hollywood, too."

5

BUT, EARL . . .

Earl Morgan, hot from the movie set of *A Matter of Love*, was in Sharo's last night. We caught the Torrid One with Crystal, the exotic and ravishing newcomer to the disco scene. Which brings up two questions and a but . . . Question number one—Where was Denise Sarno, the Torrid One's live-in throb? Question two—Is Crystal the Lady X that figures in Paramount's planned pic? Now, for the but . . . Crystal's gorgeous, Torrid One, and charming . . . BUT . . . didn't she arrive at Sharo's with none other than Sean Farrell???? Will this be just a cozy coffee klatch or do I smell T-R-O-U-B-L-E brewing?

"Now you can tell me the truth," Pat said, pushing a glob of Jell-O to one side of her tray in the noisy lunchroom. "How does he look up close?"

"He's really nice looking," Crystal answered.

"Really *nice* looking?" Pat frowned up her face. "What kind of talk is that? Is the fool as fine in person as he is in the movies, that's what I want to know."

"I guess he is," Crystal said. "I mean, like the article said, I did go with Sean, so I was a little worried when Earl asked me to dance."

"You were?" Pat's attention drifted away to a dream world of her own.

"Sean was furious!"

"He was?"

"Did you know that he was short?"

"Earl?"

"Uh-uh, Sean," Crystal said. She had brought a plastic cup of fruit salad from home for lunch and was picking out the bananas. "He's about my height."

"He's got nice eyes, though," Pat said.

"They're deeper blue than they look on television," Crystal said, smiling at her friend. "You can really tell when he's close and you look right into his eyes."

"How about Earl?" Pat wriggled in her seat. "Tell me about Earl."

"He's okay, I guess," Crystal said, pretending to examine her nails. "I mean, if you like chocolate pudding that's six foot two, a mustache, pearly white teeth, black curly hair and dimples, then he's okay."

"I think my heart just stopped," Pat said.

"I enjoy that kind of thing, but I don't let it get to me," Crystal said. "Not really."

"I'd let it get to me," Pat said. "I showed Donald your picture in the paper and you know what he said?"

"What?"

"He said it wasn't no big thing, because *his* picture was in the paper once. I asked him what his picture was in the paper for, and he come telling me about how he saved some kid from being bit by a dog, and it turned out the dog belonged to the guy that owned the newspaper."

"I don't see why you even talk to him," Crystal said.

"He's okay," Pat said. "He's so cute, and he knocks me out with his corny little love poems."

"Love poems?"

"Uh-huh. The other day he come up with something about 'Violets are blue, daisies are yellow/ My love's in bloom, since I been your fellow.'"

"And you like that childish stuff?"

"Love it to death, child," Pat said. "Here he come now with Charlie Harris from the tennis team."

The two boys, Donald and Charlie, brought their trays and sat down with Crystal and Pat.

"Yo, I got a new poem for you." Donald had a wide, toothy smile.

"Crystal doesn't want to hear your poems," Pat said.

"She don't have to listen," Donald said. "But the world *needs* this poem."

"I heard it," Charlie said. "It's pretty good."

"'My Love for You Is Like a Fire Hydrant, by Donald Evans.'" Donald was reading from a piece of theme paper.

"'My love for you is like a fire hydrant, gushing out to save you from the fire of time/ It is steady, despite the dogs of war/ And will last, now and forevermore.'"

"That's nice," Pat said, glancing at Crystal, who looked up at the ceiling.

"'My love for you is like a fire hydrant,'" Donald went on. "'Waiting on the sidewalk of your life/ Marking off the No-Parking Zone of my feelings.' The end."

"He wrote a poem about a fire hydrant?" Rowena was

doing stretching exercises in front of the mirror.

"They're so silly it's unbelievable," Crystal said. She was waiting for Jerry to finish mounting a photo montage of her that they were going to take to Marc Everby's office.

"I had this boyfriend once that was just so together," Rowena said. "I think I must have loved him more than anyone or anything else in the world."

"You broke up with him?"

"Yeah, sort of." Rowena sat up and rested her head on her knee. "Actually, I think, he broke up with me. I used to get these real deep depressions. You know, like everything is just awful and you hate yourself. I don't suppose you ever get that way, but I do."

"I think I know what you mean," Crystal said. "You're talking and no one seems to understand what you're talking about."

"Yeah, that's it," Rowena said.

"Your boyfriend didn't like that?"

"Steve—his name's Steve, and he's this really big lawyer," Rowena went on. "When I got really down, he didn't have the time to deal with me. You know what I mean? At first I was hurt and everything, but then I figured that it takes a lot of time to deal with a person when they're depressed. He said he didn't have time."

"I think that's lousy, Rowena," Crystal said.

"No, because most people don't have a lot of time. Most people have to hustle around to make it and everything and they really can't help you. If you want to be loved and everything, you got to be happy. You can't come on to people sad and depressed all the time. They can't handle it."

"Hey." Crystal put her arm around Rowena's shoulders.

"Don't touch me, I'm all sweaty," Rowena said. "You have to be perfect for Everby."

"I'm trying not to be nervous," Crystal said.

"No, it's okay, you can be nervous," Rowena said. "Men like that. It makes them feel good if you're a little scared."

"Then he should feel fine when he sees me," Crystal said, "because my stomach is doing flip-flops."

"Are we friends?" Rowena asked.

"Sure."

"Really?"

"Of course."

"I'm glad," Rowena said. "Because I think you're really nice. Sometimes in this business, you're so into being something that somebody wants you to be, you don't have time to be friends."

"We're friends," Crystal said. "We'll make the time."

"Thanks."

The door to the studio opened and Jerry Goodwin started to come in just as Crystal knelt next to Rowena. Rowena wiped her hand off on her bare thigh and took Crystal's hand in her own. The soft light from the frosted windows framed the two girls as they shared a silent moment. Jerry started to speak, thought better of it, then left the room in search of his cigarettes.

"This is the waiting room?" Crystal sat with Jerry Goodwin in the ornately designed room.

"The Blue Room is famous," Jerry said. "I mean, have you ever been in a room with blue rugs, blue curtains, a blue piano, and blue furniture before?"

"And it looks like somebody's living room," Crystal said.

"Let me tell you something about Marc Everby." Jerry lowered his voice. "The guy's the most powerful man in the magazine business. As a matter of fact, he's the most powerful man in the girlie business. If he wants a room that's all blue, that's what he's going to get."

"You said Loretta talked to him about me?"

"Yeah." Jerry turned away from Crystal, inspecting the room.

Soft music came from somewhere in the room. It sounded vaguely Spanish with lots of drums. Crystal could feel the excitement in her stomach. Part of it was from Jerry. She could tell he was nervous, too. Even the way he said *La Femme* was different. He said it with a kind of reverence.

There were pictures of girls on the wall. All of them were beautiful, most of them were nude. Crystal swallowed hard.

"What exactly did Loretta say to Mr. Everby?"

"She told him that you were young and fresh," Jerry said. "She must have been convincing, because he doesn't see many people in person."

"She said he was anxious to see me," Crystal said. "That sounds good."

"Did she tell you that he wants a new set of pictures?" Jerry asked. "Something a little fleshier?"

The music seemed farther away. Crystal glanced at Jerry, wondering what to say.

76

"I'm only sixteen," she said. "I can't . . ."

"He probably wouldn't risk anything too sexy in the magazine, but he'll want them for the magazine's files."

"Just how sexy does he mean?"

"You can always say no," Jerry said, "if that's what you want to do."

"I couldn't pose for him nude." Crystal shook her head.

"You wouldn't be posing for him," Jerry said. He put his hand on Crystal's arm. "He would get the photos, but he's not a photographer."

"I couldn't . . ."

"That's what I thought, too," Jerry said. "That's why I was disappointed that Loretta hadn't spoken to you. If you were my client, I'd of spoken to you."

"I feel like leaving right now," Crystal said. She felt the tears stinging her eyes.

"Look, Crystal, you're a big girl now. People are talking about big things for you." Jerry lifted Crystal's chin gently. "If he asks us for photographs, you owe it to yourself, I guess you even owe it to Loretta, not to make a decision right away."

"I *know* I'm not going to pose without my clothes on!" Crystal hissed.

"I'm not saying that you should," Jerry said. "All I'm saying is that you should at least see what Marc says. You weigh the benefits, you weigh what it means to you. All you have to do today is to give him a pretty smile and then you make your own decision later, okay?"

Crystal suddenly felt very small. She looked down at the rug. Out of the corner of her eye she saw a movement. It was a cat. Its long hair was actually dyed the same color as the rug. It sat, its pug face immobile, staring at Crystal.

"Mr. Everby's on his way!" The voice came from behind them. Jerry stood up quickly, and for a moment, Crystal thought that he was going to stand at attention.

Crystal turned and saw that Marc Everby's secretary was standing in the doorway, holding the door open. She was tall, a lot taller than Crystal, and the smile she wore seemed to be more a part of her face than a sign of pleasure.

It was just past noon, but Marc Everby wore a silk house-coat over his slacks. He had deep lines on the side of his face and just a touch of gray in his eyebrows.

"Jerry, good to see you."

"Good to see you, Marc." Crystal watched as the two men shook hands.

"And this is the young lady I've heard so much about?"

"Crystal, meet Marc Everby."

"How do you do?"

"I'm doing fine, just fine, young lady." Marc Everby smiled warmly.

"I was just telling Crystal that *La Femme* has been in business since long before she was born."

"I'm sure Crystal's not interested in the business side of the magazine," Marc said. He sat in a high-backed chair and crossed his legs.

"No." Jerry looked for another place to sit. "I'm sure she's not."

"You're really a fresh face," Marc said. His voice was deep, almost caressing his words as he spoke.

"Thank you."

"I can see a nice spread on you," Marc went on. "You're not bosomy enough for mid-book, but we can put you in the front of the book. You ever do any hamburger ads?"

"Hamburger ads? No," Crystal said.

"That's good," Marc said. "We're doing a layout of girls who work in fast-food places, in September, and I wouldn't want to do another hamburger girl."

"Crystal's been doing a lot of high-fashion stuff," Jerry said. "She's a mild sensation in Italy."

"Can you get the roundness out of her cheeks, Jerry?" Everby stood and crossed to where Crystal was sitting. He moved her face from side to side. "Maybe she ought to have her molars taken out."

"I don't think so," Crystal said, smiling.

"Oh, why not?"

"Well . . ." Crystal looked at Marc Everby and saw that he wasn't at all kidding. "I just never thought of it."

"That's for the people who are handling you to think about," Marc said. "You want to stand up and let me take a look at you."

Crystal stood and moved away from Marc. Then she turned slowly so that he could see her.

"She has a good figure," Jerry said. "Very nice bone structure. Good calves for a Black girl."

"Loretta said that Joe Sidney was considering her for a part in his new production?" Marc spoke to Jerry without turning his head away from Crystal.

"Crystal doesn't even know about the part yet," Jerry said.

"I'm afraid that you just let the cat out of the bag."

"You ready for stardom, Crystal?" Marc asked.

"I hope so," Crystal answered.

"You need to do more than hope in this business," Marc said. "But you're pretty enough, that's for sure. Is your body firm?"

"I think so."

"You *think* so?" Everby glanced at Jerry and shook his head. "Stand up," he said to Crystal.

Before he touched her, she knew what he was going to do. He put his hands on her stomach and squeezed gently. Then he put his hand on her back and slid it down. Crystal held her breath as Marc Everby touched her. She tried to stop thinking, as well. If only she could shut out the room for a minute. The room, and Marc Everby, and Jerry. Just for a minute.

"Send me some pictures," he said, turning away. He crossed the room in long, loping steps. "I think we can use her."

"I'm so excited I don't know what to do with myself." Jerry Goodwin hadn't spoken until the doors of the elevator had closed behind him and Crystal. "Do you realize what happened in there?"

"You mean him feeling me up?" Crystal said.

"You made an impression on Marc Everby! We're going to be in *La Femme*!" Jerry put both hands to his head. "Marc Everby wants to use you in a layout!"

"That's good," Crystal said, without feeling any of the emotion that Jerry was showing.

"You in the mood to go someplace and celebrate?" Jerry asked.

"I think I'm going to head home."

"Okay, look, I'll call Loretta. What I want to do is to get you over to the studio as soon as possible. Maybe even tomorrow. We shoot as much as possible. We don't want to blow this chance. Right?"

"Right."

"And Crystal?"

"Yeah."

"Look, I just want to tell you that you were a real pro in there." Jerry put his hands on her shoulders. "Sometimes this business gets a little rough around the edges, but you handled it well. I'll call you tomorrow, or maybe Loretta will call you, okay?"

"Sure."

Crystal hurried home. It was cool and there were a few drops of rain falling. The sky was gray but bright, almost silver. When she got home, her mother was cooking. The hearty smell of the beef stew filled the kichen.

"How did it go?" Crystal's mother had tasted the stew and held the wooden spoon inches from her mouth.

"Okay, I guess," Crystal said. "That Marc Everby's got some office."

"Did you actually meet him?" Her mother turned and leaned against the table.

"Yes," Crystal said. "I didn't think he was so great, though."

"Oh, he is!" Carol Brown said. She sat at the kitchen table. "He's simply fabulous! Sit down and tell me about the meeting!"

"Well . . ." Crystal sat at the end of the table. "First he kept us waiting forever."

"He's probably got a thousand things to do," her mother said. "I understand he runs that magazine with an iron hand. That's why it's been around so long."

"He said that maybe I should have my molars taken out," Crystal said. "He was serious, too!"

"It's because your face is so round" was the quick reply. "You want something to eat?"

"No."

"I think by next year you'll lose that roundness," her mother said. "It's not that bad, anyway. You'll have to watch your diet, though."

"Then he asked me to stand up and turn around, so he could look at me."

"Did you feel beautiful?"

"Not exactly."

"You have to think beautiful at times like that, Crystal," her mother said. "You have to tell yourself that you're beautiful, and then project it."

"He put his hands on my stomach."

"You have a good body, I'm sure he could tell that. And you'll keep it a long time, too. My mother kept her body, the firmness, until she was well into her thirties. Even with three children she was considered the prettiest Black woman in Beckley," her mother said. "Did he say when he'd make a decision?"

"He told Jerry to send over some photos," Crystal said. "He thinks maybe he can use me in a layout."

"Oh, my God!" Crystal's mother put her hand on her daughter's arm. "You mean he's actually going to . . . ?"

"I guess so," Crystal said. "Jerry was really excited about it."

"Baby, it's wonderful! It's simply wonderful!"

"I guess it is," Crystal said.

"Look, what do you say we turn off this stew and go out for dinner tonight? Let's party!"

"Mama, I'm tired. I'm really so tired. I've got to shower, too. I feel dirty."

"Okay, dear," her mother said. "I'm sure it's been a hard day for you."

"What . . . what do you think about him putting his hands on me?" Crystal asked.

"It's his business to judge girls," Carol Brown said. "To him it's probably no different than checking out the feel of a typewriter. People like him don't even think of you as a girl. They think of you as part of their business."

"I guess that's how I felt, too," Crystal said.

"That's because you're getting to be quite the professional."

The water felt good. Crystal had it as hot as she could stand it. She closed her eyes and imagined she was in a steaming pool somewhere far away. Perhaps it was a lush tropical island. There would be birds sitting in the trees above her. Maybe there would be a fawn prancing nearby. Yes, that would be all. Just the fawn, a few birds, and her.

She thought about standing in Marc Everby's office. She remembered him walking toward her, *knowing* that he would touch her. She almost knew how it would feel to have his hands on her.

Quickly she forced her mind back to her jungle paradise. She washed slowly, shutting everything out of her mind.

"Okay, so here's the deal." Pat sat across from Crystal in the library. "I want you to double-date with me and Donald and Charlie."

"With who?"

"You know Donald and Charlie," Pat said. "Charlie's nice."

"He might be nice but I don't know him, and why would I want to go out with him even if I did know him?"

"Because my mother's not going to let me go out with Donald by myself. She met Donald once and she knows Charlie's mother. And she knows you. So, either you go out with me and Donald and Charlie or I can't go out at all."

"You're not that desperate for a date, Pat."

"Girl, don't tell me how desperate I am. I am sixteen years old and have never, mind you, never been on a date with a real live boy. My mother doesn't think I should go on a date until I finish high school."

"What so magical about finishing high school?"

"That's what I asked my mother," Pat said. "And she wanted to know why I was so anxious to go on a date and what did I think I would be doing?"

"So what did you tell her?"

"I *told* her," Pat said, "that I wanted to double-date with you because we were best friends. What I was *thinking* was that I didn't know what I would be doing, but I sure wanted to find out."

"I don't date," Crystal answered. "Unless you call that creep, Sean Farrell, a date."

"I'd die to go out with Sean Farrell, even if he is a creep. There's nothing wrong with a good-looking creep now and then."

"I'll think about it," Crystal said.

"You want to think about it before Friday?" Pat said. "I kind of told my mother we were going out together Friday night."

"Pat, you are a mess. Suppose my parents say no?"

"They'll say yes," Pat said. "And anyway, if I don't start dating soon I'm going to be a bigger mess."

"It's all in your head," Crystal said.

"No, it ain't, it's in my Social Studies class. You know who's checking Donald out?"

"Who?"

"You know that skinny chick who thinks she looks like Tina Turner?"

"That Mavis somebody? The one who runs around in those little short dresses?"

"Her. She was throwing herself all up in his face and everything."

"Why? Donald's not that cute."

"Yes, he is, Crissie," Pat said. "I think he's cute."

"Yeah, but you're in love with the dude. You throw out that love and what you got? He's sweet, but that's about all."

"I think he's cute, and now that he's playing flute with

Tito's combo, everybody's checking him out."

"You told me Donald only played classical music," Crystal said. "Tito doesn't play classical. He plays that salsa."

"Donald is getting into it, too," Pat said. "He's really good. That's why Miss Thing is chasing him. And from what I hear, she'll do *anything* to get a guy."

"I got to check with Mama," Crystal said. "Where we supposed to be going Friday night?"

"To this club that Donald says is really hot. And then I got to be home at twelve o'clock. I think my mama got a Cinderella complex."

"And who am I supposed to be? Your fairy godmother?"

"And Donald will be my Prince Charming."

"With his dumb-butt poetry?"

"With his dumb-butt poetry." Pat sighed.

Crystal had picked up a copy of *La Femme* on the way home from school. She lay across her bed, thumbing slowly through the pages. The girls in the magazine were beautiful. She looked closely at some of the pictures and saw that they had been shot with either a soft focus or developed that way. Loretta had told her about a model who started developing wrinkles around her eyes and the account photographer had used softer and softer focus to keep her career going.

She knew boys in her school liked *La Femme*. They would sure buy it if they knew she was in it. Crystal looked at the faces of the girls. They were all supposed to be scientists. They looked happy enough, as if they enjoyed showing their bodies. Crystal could look at them, look at their smiles, and imagine that it was all right to pose the way they were. But when she imagined herself doing it, lying back on a couch with her legs . . . No, she couldn't imagine it at all.

"Crystal?"

"Who is it?" Crystal pushed the copy of *La Femme* between her bed and the wall.

"It's me, Sister Gibbs. I got something for you."

"Come on in." Crystal sat up quickly and dabbed cleansing cream on her face to hide the places where tears had smeared her makeup.

"Look."

Crystal turned and saw Sister Gibbs bring her hands from behind her back. In the palm of her right hand was an orange puffy ball.

"A kitten?" Crystal stood up to take a closer look.

"I was walking down near that pet shop over on Fulton Street, down from Concord Baptist, and I seed this crowd, so I went over and took me a look. Guess what the fools got in the window?"

"What?"

"They got this little kitty in a cage with a snake."

"With a snake?"

"Yeah, child." Sister Gibbs sat heavily on the end of the bed. "Poor thing is trembling and shaking to beat all get-out. I marched myself right in there and asked them fools what in God's name they was doing. They come talking about how they putting on a show so they can sell them some snakes."

"They were going to let the snake eat this kitten?"

"Sure as I'm sitting here." Sister Gibbs rested her elbows

on her knees. "Now if that ain't Satan's handiwork, ain't nothing is! You hear me?"

"I hear you, Sister Gibbs."

"I snatched that kitty up and said if they don't stop they evil ways I'm going right down to the S.P.C.A. and run 'em out of business!"

"People do anything for a dollar."

"You want that kitty?"

"I sure do," Crystal said. "Does he have a name?"

"None I know of," Sister Gibbs said.

"I'll call him Gizmo, then," Crystal said, taking the tiny kitten.

"Gizmo?" What kind of name is that for a cat?"

"It just came to me," Crystal said. "You don't like it?"

"I guess it's okay," Sister Gibbs said. "You know what happened to me yesterday?"

"What?"

"I was doing me some day's work for this White girl over on Ninety-third Street and I was catching my breath a little when I seed her reading the paper. I look at the paper and then I look again. Then I said to myself, 'Ain't that my Crystal in the paper?' Well, sure 'nough it was. So I told this White girl I knowed you. She didn't say nothing, but she give me one of them looks like to turn hard cheese into buttermilk, like she don't believe a word I be saying.

"Now, nothin' I like better'n Jesus Christ A-Mighty and I follow His ways. I don't be going around here lying— Watch that kitty 'fore he pee on your bed, sweetheart."

Crystal took a hatbox from the bottom of her closet and put

Gizmo in it. "He'll be a fashion cat," she said.

"So when this poor skinny thing look at me like I'm lying, I look right back at her and say, 'As God is my Secret Judge, I know that girl.'

"You know what she say?"

"What?"

Sister Gibbs pursed large lips into as small and as tight a pout as she could and mimicked the girl she had been working for. "She said, 'Well, why don't you bring her around sometime.' Well, what she say that for? I told her that Crystal Brown don't be coming to no *ordinary* places like this. I would have said no second-class places, but I need them few dollars I get from her. Then I said I'd bring an autographed picture tomorrow. Which is today."

"Sister Gibbs, you are too much!" Crystal said.

"You got to be as much as you can or these people will run over you and think they doing you a favor!"

Crystal got an eight-by-ten glossy from her desk and signed it "My best friend, Sister Gibbs."

"There," she said. "That should do it."

"And who this boy your mama saying you going out with tonight?"

"Charlie Harris. He's on the tennis team. He's really a friend of Pat's boyfriend."

"Pat's still saved, ain't she?"

"Uh-huh." Crystal was taking off the cream with a sponge.

"Your mama don't seem too happy with your going out with these boys."

"You know how Mama is," Crystal said. "They're not in show business or anything."

"What time you planning to be home?"

"Pat's got to be home by twelve, so I'll be home around that time, too."

"You want me to take care of—what you call him?"

"Gizmo. We have to get a litter box for him and some cat food," Crystal said.

"I know how to take care of a cat, girl!" Sister Gibbs said. "They didn't make me with this morning's coffee, you know."

"Go *on* with your bad self, Sister Gibbs."

"EVERBY'S PAYING JERRY FOR THE SHOOTING SESSION," Loretta said as she, Crystal, and Crystal's mother sat in her office. "The thing is that *La Femme* gets to keep all of the pictures that he turns over to them. Which means that they might show up in their European edition, but that's no real problem."

"Do you like Everby?" Crystal asked.

"No, I think he's a pig," Loretta said. "But he's a very influential pig, and he's a very useful pig if you know what you're doing, which is why I called you over here today. Carol, can I get you coffee or anything?"

"No, thank you."

"I've asked you both here to discuss Crystal's career. She can go a number of ways, some a lot more promising than others." Loretta went on, "She can work fairly steadily as an all-around girl and make a fairly decent living. She'll have the same struggle that White models have with the added burden that there just aren't as many calls for Black models. Many agencies won't even take on a new Black model's bookings if they already have one. It just doesn't pay. It doesn't mean that she's not beautiful or that she's not a very good model."

"But aren't there exceptions?"

Crystal turned away from the anxiety on her mother's face.

"Any model that makes it really big is an exception," Loretta said. "And, yes, there are Black models who have made it big. Shari Belafonte comes to mind, Naomi Sims, Iman, Gerry Maxwell, Joyce Smith, and a few others. But *very* few others. What Crystal needs is a big push."

"That's where you think this movie will come in?" Carol Brown asked.

"I think so," Loretta said. "If the movie is a hit we can go the Hollywood route, but even if it's not, it should be enough to give Crystal the kind of push she needs. Just the fact that accounts think that consumers will identify her with Hollywood is worth a lot."

"And this is a comedy?"

"It's a romantic comedy," Loretta said. "Three American girls, two White and one Black, are on vacation in Europe. A letter is delivered to their room by mistake. It's supposedly a bitter letter from a lawyer who regretfully says that a certain person has inherited a title and several million pounds. The girls look for this guy in the hotel and find that he's a dishwasher and has no idea that he's inherited the money. They agree to take turns pursuing him. Of course, it ends up that he planted the letter and so it's all good fun.

"Originally the part was written with a Spanish girl in mind, but one of the backers wanted a Black girl. She's supposed to be naïve, kittenish, and a little awkward, so Sidney doesn't think the acting will be a problem."

"It certainly sounds good," Carol said.

"It sounds wonderful," Loretta said. "But let's know what we're going into. There's still a chance that Joe Sidney will choose somebody else."

"I thought you said that he liked me from the photos."

"He did," Loretta said. "But with these Hollywood types that doesn't mean much. He likes you because he thinks you're hot and he can convince the bankers to give him the money to make the films. If he can't get the guarantees he needs with you, and he can get them with somebody else, he'll go with the somebody else. If we get the spread in *La Femme*, and he sees where he can get some free publicity, he'll like you a lot more."

"It's a chance, but I think it's a worthwhile chance, don't you think so, Crystal?" Carol Brown asked.

"It also might mean a lot of smiling when you don't feel like smiling, and some awkward situations that you'll have to handle."

"Crystal can handle herself," Carol said quickly. "You mentioned something about a line of dresses?"

"Dresses? Oh, yes, Perigord is a new French line. They want Crystal if she gets the spread in *La Femme*. I'm asking for a flat ten thousand dollars per month for the six-month campaign they have in mind plus ten thousand a month for every month that the film is showing under the original distributorship."

"They'll pay that much?" Crystal asked.

"It's a gamble," Loretta said. "If you get the part, and if the movie's a smash, they're getting over like crazy. But from our point of view, if you sign with them, it means that you won't be getting other clothing accounts for a while."

"That's a lot of money," Crystal said.

"Honey, look at me." Loretta leaned across the desk. "Chances don't come very often in this business—or in life. I'm sure your mother has told you that. Once in a while, in a very few lives, a great opportunity comes along. Think of yourself as a feast. Everybody is going to want a part of you, but you know it won't last forever. So you have to take what you can get while it does last. You have to think like a taker. Is that going to be hard for you?"

"I'll manage," Crystal said, looking at her mother.

"I'm sure you will," Loretta said. "And now I have to go out and find a ten-year-old boy who looks like he's five for a toy account. So if you'll excuse me . . ."

Crystal and her mother walked crosstown toward the subway line. The streets along the way bustled with the commercial life of the city. Cars honked and nudged their way through crowds of pedestrians, delivery men moved with sure swiftness, handling their packages, moving in and out of buildings like athletes in an arena of concrete and glass.

"I'm really excited for you, Crystal," Carol said as they waited for a light at Lexington Avenue. "You're actually doing something with your life. Something so wonderful, I dream about it at night. Sometimes I feel that you're doing it as much for me as for yourself. And I'm grateful."

"I'm excited, too," Crystal said. "But sometimes I don't know how to think about the things going on. You know what I mean? It's so new. People talking about money, and—what did Loretta say?—thinking about myself as a 'feast.' It's almost as if they're talking another language. As if they're saying one thing and meaning something else."

"That's the beauty of it," Carol said as a taxi turned in to the crosswalk and blocked it, making them walk in the middle of the street. "They are talking another language. It's the language of success. You don't hear that too much, I'm afraid. You're taking a chance. You don't get anywhere by not taking chances."

"Right," Crystal said. "Right."

Pat came to Crystal's house to wait for the boys. Pat told Crystal that Donald was taking them to a place called Los Hermanos. On the way out she had stopped and told her mother that she wouldn't be home late.

"I'm surprised," Carol Brown had said, "that you're going out at all with these young men."

Crystal had smiled, but the remark had bothered her. It was clear that her mother didn't think much of either Donald or Charlie. She hoped the place they were going to would be nice, to prove her mother wrong. It wasn't.

"Normally you got to be eighteen to get in here, but the owner knows me," Donald said.

"He probably knows the police, too," Pat said. "This place is terrible looking!"

"You sure this is where we want to go, man?" Charlie asked.

"Yeah," Donald said. "This band that's playing here is going to be playing in a big jazz club on Broadway next week, and then it's going to cost twenty-five dollars *apiece* just to walk in the place."

"What do you think, Crissie?"

"Let's go in," Crystal said. What she was thinking was that she was overdressed. Donald wore a dark suit with a sweater, and Charlie wore slacks and a blazer with sleeves that were at least an inch too short. Pat had worn a simple little dress with a bit of material draped on one side, the kind that so many girls from the church called their "party" dress.

Crystal had worn a Norma Kamali dress a buyer at Altman's had given her at a large discount. She had also done too good a job on her makeup. She could tell it in Pat's eyes when she saw her.

Maybe her mother was right, she thought. Doing her face just so was part of her life now. The way she dressed was part of her life, too. And as much as she liked Pat, the girl who had been her best friend for so long was not as important a part of her life as she had been.

Los Hermanos was a Brazilian club and restaurant. The decor was simple with a real feeling of South America, and the accents of the thin waiters pleasing. As it turned out, the owner didn't know Donald at all, but he did know his father.

He whispered something to one of the waiters, who promptly took the wine list off the table.

"The inside of this place looks nicer than the outside," Charlie observed.

"It's okay," Pat said.

"The Big 'D' don't take his friends to no chump places," Donald said.

"Is that you?" Crystal asked. "The Big 'D'?"

"He's always trying to get some cool tag for himself," Pat said. "He said he used to be called 'Icing' 'cause he's so sweet."

"Hey, that's what the ladies were calling me," Donald said.

"*What* ladies?" Pat asked, an eyebrow properly arched.

They ordered, with Pat and Crystal both choosing *Pollo Portuguesa* and Charlie and Donald ordering shrimp with green sauce.

"I got to admit that this is a nice place," Charlie said.

"It'll do," Crystal said. "The food's cheap, anyway."

"Cheap?" Charlie looked at her. "That *Pollo* thing you and Pat ordered was the cheapest thing they had, and that was eight-ninety-five!"

"If you say so," Crystal said, glancing toward Pat.

"So how's the tennis going?" Pat asked Charlie.

"It's going okay," Charlie said. "The coach said that if I can get my backhand together he'll see about getting me into some outside tournaments."

"You going to play against John McEnroe?" Crystal asked.

"He's going to be John McEnroe's ball boy," Pat said as a white-coated busboy put bread on the table.

Charlie made a fist and shook it at Pat. "I'm going to have to knock you out, woman, if you don't stop putting down my game!"

"You ever see Charlie play?" Donald asked Crystal.

"No."

"Hey, he's good!" Donald said.

"You got to come check me out sometime." Charlie leaned away from the table. "I'm playing against Stuyvesant next week, and they got this Vietnamese guy who's supposed to be pretty good. You can come and see me wipe him out."

"If he beats him, I'm going to write one of those 'Rocky'-type numbers for him," Donald said.

"Then every time he comes onto the court, the band can play it," Crystal said.

"Only the band doesn't go to games, so Donald's going to hum it real loud from the bleachers."

Crystal laughed with the others. She was surprised at how easily Pat made jokes.

The waiter delivered the food with a great flourish. There was rice and a bowl of black beans—*frijoles negro*, Donald called them—and the owner sent a plate of hors d'oeuvres as well.

The band was made up of four players: a pianist, a guitarist, a drummer, and the leader, who sang and played flute. They introduced the numbers in Portuguese and played gentle sambas that caught Crystal in their easy rhythms.

After several couples had begun to dance, Donald asked Pat and they went out on the floor.

"You and Pat been friends a long time?" Charlie asked.

"Since the second grade," Crystal said. "That's when she started going to the same church I go to."

"She told me you were going to be in a movie." There was a flake of crust half the size of a dime on Charlie's chin, which Crystal tried to ignore.

"It looks like I've got the part," Crystal said.

"You like actor-type guys?" Charlie asked.

"As opposed to what other kinds of guys?" Crystal asked.

Charlie took a large mouthful of his shrimps and managed to get a drop of sauce precisely on the bread crumb on his chin.

"There are lots of different-type guys," Charlie said. "Doctors, lawyers, athletes."

"It depends on the guy, I guess," Crystal said.

Charlie flicked at the crumb with his tongue and missed it.

"Yeah, I guess so."

"What kind of guy are you?"

"I'm an athlete," Charlie said. "My mom wants me to get into law, but I figure I got time for that."

"Oh, I see."

Crystal watched Charlie flick at the crumb with his tongue again. This time he dislodged it and it fell onto his collar. Crystal suppressed a laugh into a smile as Donald and Pat got back to the table.

"I see you people are having a good time," Pat said.

"We're doing okay," Charlie said.

"Half the people in this place are Black, and they're all speaking Spanish," Donald said.

"They're speaking Portuguese," Crystal said. "It's almost like Spanish."

"You people going to dance?" Pat asked.

"No one's asked me," Crystal said, looking at her fingernails.

"Okay, you want to dance?" Donald asked.

"Not you, fool!" Pat gave Donald a shove with her elbow that sent the fork full of black beans in his hand into Charlie's lap.

"Yo, man, what you doing?" Charlie moved his chair away quickly and picked the beans off his lap. "These pants cost three dollars to get out the cleaner's!"

"It was Pat's fault," Donald said. "She bumped my arm!"

"Come on, you want to dance?" Crystal took the fork from Charlie's hand and put it on the edge of his plate.

"No!"

"Oh, go on, Charlie," Pat said. "Don't be a grump."

"I don't want to dance!"

"Please." Crystal put her hand on Charlie's arm.

"Come on," he said reluctantly.

Crystal knew something was wrong when Charlie put the wrong arm around her. She switched arms easily enough but when he started cranking her right hand up and down as if he were pumping water, and she felt his knees banging against her legs, she cracked up completely. Charlie Harris, athlete type, couldn't dance a lick.

"So how was your big date?" Crystal's father looked up from

his racing form to the clock over the stove. It was eleven-forty-five.

"The guy was a real . . ." Crystal searched for a word. "A cute nerd is what he was."

"Bad time, huh?"

"No." Crystal sat at the table and put her chin on her hands. "Good time, really. You know, Pat's really fun to go out with. And Donald is as crazy as they come."

"So what did you do?" Daniel Brown closed the paper.

"We went to this club; it's called Los Hermanos. Kind of a nice place. We had dinner—Portuguese food, which is nice—and then we danced. At least Donald, Pat, and I danced, because Charlie—that's the guy I was supposed to be with—couldn't dance."

"He Black?"

"Yep. I asked him how he could play tennis, that's his big thing, and move around a dance floor so badly," Crystal said. "At first he got kind of mad because we were laughing at him, but then he came around. Then Donald gets the idea that we should go to Central Park and take a ride in one of those carriages."

"You ain't got to have no rhythm to play tennis." Daniel put his feet up on the table. "Now, if you playing basketball, you got to have rhythm."

"He wants me to come see him play in a match," Crystal said. "Maybe I'll go if I can find the time. I don't think he's got a lot of money for dates."

"He bring you home in a cab?"

"We took a cab from the subway," Crystal said.

"Seems like you had a nice time, though."

"I did," Crystal said. "I can't tell why, but I did."

"I like it when I see you smiling like that," her father said. "I haven't seen that smile for a long time."

"You've got to be kidding," Crystal said. "I'm always smiling."

"Yeah, but lately your smiles look like you're thirty-six instead of sixteen."

"Why is it that fathers always want us to be little girls?" Crystal asked. "At least Mom realizes I can't stay a baby forever. Is there any soda left?"

"Yeah, there's some—enough for a glass or two," Daniel said. Crystal saw that his expression had changed.

"I was only kidding, Daddy, honest."

"I know you were, baby," he said. "But there's a reason I want you to stay a little girl. You know, having a child ain't that easy. The way I figure, if I raise you like I've done everything else in life, I'll screw half of it up. So the longer you stay a little girl, the longer I'll have to see where I'm messing it up, and I'll have a shot at making things right."

"You're serious, aren't you?" Crystal took the soda out of the refrigerator and poured a glass. "You want some soda?"

"Yeah, I'm serious," her father said. "And, no, I don't want no soda. Reach back there behind the milk and get me a can of beer."

"Daddy, you're okay," Crystal said. "I think you're a good father. That's what counts, isn't it?"

"How I know?" Daniel asked. "I ain't never had no children before. But you know what I figured out?"

"What?"

"I ain't saying it's right or nothing." Her father popped the top of the beer. "I figured what I want is to give you something. You know, like you a gunfighter going out to meet the world. I'd like to give you a special gun, or a trick draw or something. Get you ready."

"Crystal Brown, gunfighter!" Crystal took an imaginary draw. "I like it!"

"When I was a kid and things used to go wrong, I used to go sit in Marcus Garvey Park. I remember one time my Daddy had come home, and I asked him for money to buy some new sneakers. He said something about not having any money, and I got hot and said he never had no money.

"He up and popped me one, and I went out the house mad as anything. I went out and sat in the park all night long. While I was sitting there I thought about being a gunfighter. That was my secret ambition, to be a cowboy."

"You? A cowboy?"

"Yeah, a lot of men have these little things they want to do but can't talk about. Me, I always wanted to be a cowboy. I could see myself riding on a big white horse, carrying a guitar and everything. But when I was mad, then I would be a gunfighter. I'd imagine I was a gunfighter. I'd have this special draw and nobody would mess with me. Lucky for me, I never got my hands on a real gun, or I'd of probably spent half my life in some jail."

"And you'd sit in the park and think about things like that?"

"The park was special to me. It was a place I could go

102

when things weren't working out for me. That night my father popped me I sat in the park and thought about being a gunfighter. I figured if I had lived in the old West he could have taught me how to shoot a gun, and then I wouldn't have to ask him for sneakers and stuff. Later, when I got to be a man, I knew why he popped me. I had asked him for money and he didn't have it, and it hurts to have a kid ask you for something and you can't give it to them. It really does."

"I think you've given me just about everything I've ever wanted," Crystal said.

"I haven't given you nothing to get you over," her father said. "What you got you got from God. I'd like to get you that fast draw I was talking about. Something. But it's just not that simple anymore. I try to tell you what I know about life, stuff like that, but it don't work, because most of the stuff I'm telling you got to do with my life and my world, and there ain't no way in the world you can understand it."

"I understand what you say to me, Daddy," Crystal protested.

"I think you understand that I mean well," her father said. "I'm caught between a poor man's dream and a rich man's nightmare and afraid to let either one of them go. You're young enough and smart enough to dream things that wouldn't even fit in my head."

"I still think you're a good father," Crystal said.

"Yeah, maybe." The vein in Daniel Brown's forehead bulged as he swallowed hard. "You happy with this movie thing?"

"Yes," Crystal said. "I think it's going to be good."

"If it's what you want, then it's what I want for you."

"I still might not get the part, though."

"That's because that producer hasn't seen you the way I have. As fine as he thinks you are, he should have seen your face when you got home tonight after being with that—what did you call him?"

"Cute nerd?"

"Yeah. I bet he hasn't seen you look that good."

"I bet," Crystal said, stopping at the doorway to the kitchen before going to her room, "that you weren't a cute nerd."

"Nerd? Me? I was a killer!" Daniel Brown said. "A stone killer-diller!"

Crystal washed quickly and went to bed. She was tired, very tired. But she was happy. She hadn't liked Charlie Harris that much, and Donald was silly. But she and Pat had had a good time. She hadn't felt as good in weeks. Gizmo was on her bed, and she pushed him over to the other pillow.

7

THE MIDTOWN-MANHATTAN STUDIO LOOKED A LOT BETter than Jerry's. There were wires running all over the floor, and a small army of aluminum reflectors had been strategically placed about the high-ceilinged room.

"Crystal, did Loretta tell you how long the session would be?"

"She said it might last all day," Crystal said. She tilted her chin slightly so that Frankie Mazzaro could put highlights over her eyes from behind her.

"This is a chance in a lifetime," Jerry said. "And what we want to do is to get pictures which are going to say a lot about you, who you are, and which are going to knock Everby's eyes out."

"Why are we using this studio?" The two-piece bathing suit Crystal wore was almost the same color as her skin.

"It's better equipped than mine," Jerry said. "I worked with Mel Kaplan, the guy who owns this place, all day yesterday to get the feel of it. It's going to work out just fine."

"Did you know that I took some test shots with him once? They're in my portfolio. I took them over there." Crystal motioned toward a carousel of backdrops in the center of the studio. There was a beach scene, an outdoor Western scene, and two city scenes and others on rollers.

"We're going to use this city scene first," Jerry said. The backdrop had the outlines of tall buildings lit up at night. "I'm going to put you at a table as if you're waiting for someone in a restaurant. The theme will be the same in all the pictures, that you're young and you don't want to wait."

"Don't want to wait for what?"

"For anything," Jerry said. "How long you going to be, Frankie?"

"Just finished," Frankie said. He stood directly behind Crystal and looked at her in the mirror. Crystal looked up at his reflection, and when their eyes met, he smiled. "She's beautiful. The only thing she has to worry about is perspiration. She gets a little moist around her upper lip."

"Can she fix it herself?"

"Sure," Frankie said. "Crystal, I'm leaving all of your stuff here for you. Just watch for perspiration. *Don't* touch the highlights, all right?"

"As soon as you leave, I'm re-doing my whole face," Crystal said, smiling.

"If you do, Jerry will kill you, and then I'll come back and kill you all over again. Now be sweet!"

"Yes, Frankie."

"*Yes*, Crystal."

Frankie gathered the rest of his materials and left.

"What do you think of that guy?" Jerry asked.

"Frankie? Frankie's nice," Crystal said.

"He is." Jerry leaned against the dressing table. "You like everybody, don't you?"

"Unless I have a reason not to," Crystal said.

"You ready?"

"What am I going to be doing?"

"First, I want you to tell me what Everby's paying for."

"The pictures?"

"Why the pictures of you, though?"

Crystal shrugged. "Because he likes the way I look, I guess," she said. "That's what you said."

"He likes the way you look," Jerry said. "But it all gets back to mood. That's why you're a model. You create a mood. You can make things happen. An actress does the same thing,

106

except she has words she can use, gestures. If she feels good she can say she feels good and that helps. In print you don't speak. You have to say everything with mood."

"And I'm supposed to be sexy, right?"

"Are you sexy?"

"I think I look pretty sexy."

"That wasn't the question," Jerry said. "The question was *are* you sexy?"

"Yeah."

"How sexy?"

"Smokin'!"

"We're talking about a career, right?"

"A career," Crystal said.

"And you know what this whole thing means to me. It means big bucks down the line."

"Big bucks," Crystal said. "I know what it means."

"Okay, we'll see," Jerry said. "I told you what you're going to be dressed in, right?"

"The fur coats."

"Right, and please don't drag them along the floor. I don't want to have to pay a cleaning bill."

"Okay, you want me to start now?"

"Fine, get the bathing suit off and slip into the silver fox."

Crystal stood and then stopped near the chair. "Get the bathing suit off? I thought I was supposed to wear the bathing suit under the coat?"

"You mean you'll be nice and covered up and then you'll put on your sexy face and that's it, right?"

"I didn't say that was *it*," Crystal said.

"Well, what are you saying?"

"Why do I have to take the bathing suit off if nobody can see under the fur coat, anyway?"

"How sexy are you going to feel with the bathing suit under the coat?" Jerry asked. "Do you know what sex is all about?"

"Yes."

"What?"

"I know!"

"You know? You can't even say it."

"It's about doing it, okay?"

"No, it's not about *doing it*!" Jerry said. "Not for us. You make out in the backseat of a car, and nobody is going to buy that. Nobody is going to pay you for that. You have sex in your house, and nobody cares."

"Then what is it about?"

"It's about guys seeing a bare leg sticking out from a fur coat and looking at your face and imagining you're sending them messages. They feel good; they buy the magazine. Everby makes money."

"I don't think I should take my clothes off," Crystal said. "Why . . . why didn't you want my mother here? Loretta said you didn't want my mother here."

"You think you can make somebody want to run up and rip your clothes off if you're sitting here with a bathing suit on and your mama sitting over there watching the whole thing?"

Crystal sat down. "I don't want anybody wanting to rip my clothes off," she said.

"That's what they're paying you for, Crystal." Jerry spoke quietly. "They didn't go out there and find some ugly girl to pose. You know that. They don't get fat old ladies to pose in *La Femme*."

"I still don't think I want to take my clothes off," Crystal said.

"No problem." Jerry went to a bench and picked up a camera. "As long as you know what we're trying to do here. I'm sure you'll do your best."

Crystal took a deep breath and went to the rack where the three coats hung. She took the silver one, letting her fingers run through the soft fur. She slipped the coat on and looked at Jerry. "You want me to button it or just hold it closed."

"Whichever way you feel best," Jerry said.

Crystal closed the coat and fastened one of the buttons. She sat in the chair at the table and turned toward Jerry. On the table was a bottle of wine with a single black rose in it. She didn't feel good. Somehow she had pushed the sex part of it out of her mind. She had told herself that she was beautiful and believed it. But what did it mean? What did it mean when people, when men, were impressed enough with it to pay for it?

"Okay, now, look sexy," Jerry said. His voice was flat. He moved toward Crystal with a light meter, took a reading off her face and then off the coat. He adjusted the lights. He measured the coat again, then the face again, and looked at Crystal through the lens of the camera.

"You're bored—and sexy," Jerry said. "Keep that in mind."

The camera clicked again and again as Jerry took pictures. Crystal moved, changing positions so that the angle would be different for each shot. She closed her eyes and then opened them halfway. She parted her lips slightly. She knew how she looked. That's what being a model was, knowing how she looked, looking the way the photographer wanted her to.

The camera clicking, the motor transporting the film between each shot set up a steady rhythm.

"Put your leg out," Jerry said.

Crystal put out a leg, holding the coat closed with her hand away from the camera so that the bathing suit wouldn't show.

She bent the leg. She turned and put them both out.

"Shall I stand?"

"If you want to," Jerry said.

Crystal stood for a few pictures, but it didn't feel comfortable. She sat again.

"You want to drop the coat from your shoulders?"

Crystal let the coat slide down her shoulder. The lens on the 35-millimeter camera clicked. The motor whirred.

"Try the next coat." As Crystal went for the next coat Jerry adjusted the lighting.

The black coat was heavier, and she felt nice in it. It was luxurious and made her feel important. Jerry changed the backdrop. The table with the black rose was now in front of a backdrop of snow-covered mountains.

Jerry was still using the 35-millimeter camera.

"Try turning the chair around," Jerry said.

Crystal stood and turned the chair around. She tried the same poses with the right side of her face nearest the camera, but it didn't feel right.

"I feel awkward from this side," she said.

"Okay, change it back," Jerry said. "Let's get a little more smiling in the pictures, too."

Crystal changed the chair back, then sat on it, and crossed her legs. She leaned forward.

"The sleeve is hanging over your thigh," Jerry said. "It would help if we could see more thigh."

The camera clicked and whirred.

"How do you think we're doing?" Crystal asked.

"I don't know. How do you think we're doing?"

"I don't know, either," Crystal said.

"You want to rest for a while?"

"We've just started," Crystal said.

"Okay, let's keep at it, then," Jerry said. He spoke quietly, slowly. "Sometimes you really can't tell what you're getting until you see the proofs."

The camera clicked, whirred.

"I shot my landlady yesterday," Jerry went on. "I think if the pictures come out the way she wants she won't raise my rent."

"I hope they come out," Crystal said. She turned toward the camera and put both legs before her.

"Let's switch from the table," Jerry said. He moved the table away, and when Crystal stood, the chair as well. "Sit on the log, it's sturdy enough."

Crystal sat on the log and found that it was too low for her.

"I can't get my legs in a good position," she said.

"Just sit with your knees together and your hands on your chin," Jerry said. "Don't put your hands on your face, because I don't want your makeup smudged."

Crystal leaned forward with her knees together and her chin on her hands.

"I feel like I'm sitting on the john," she said.

"That'll probably turn some people on," Jerry said.

"That's disgusting!" Crystal smiled.

"It's disgusting that everybody isn't beautiful and handsome and rich," Jerry said. He moved in for a close shot. "But we aren't, so we spend our lives looking at people who are and dreaming."

"That's not my fault," Crystal said. Her teeth were clenched in a smile as she spoke.

"I think this works better than the table," Jerry said. "The set's a little more interesting. It has more textures. Relax for a moment while I set up the Bronica."

The Bronica stood on a tripod twenty feet from the set. It had been sitting there since Crystal arrived. It was as if it knew that it was the main camera, that it was waiting.

"How do you feel now?" Jerry said. "Better?"

"I didn't feel bad before," Crystal said.

"I thought you did," Jerry said.

"You think the pictures are coming out bad?"

"We'll see," Jerry said, flatly. "Look, try on the white coat. Maybe we can get something going with that."

"Can I have a minute?"

Jerry looked up from the camera. "A minute? Yeah, sure. You know where the washroom is."

Crystal got up from the log and stepped out of the set. Jerry went to the phone and started dialing as Crystal went to the washroom.

She knew it was going wrong. She didn't feel that the session was working. Jerry wasn't saying much; he wasn't being very encouraging at all. She didn't feel beautiful or even pretty. She wasn't feeling sexy, either.

One of her first jobs had been modeling wide fabric belts with another girl. The belts were elastic and had brass catches in the back that left marks on her ribs. She had been uncomfortable the entire session, and she hadn't done a very good job. The client had watched the shoot and kept saying she should be sexier. Afterward, she had asked the other girl how she managed to look so sexy.

"Just forget who you really are," the girl had said. "Make believe you're some kind of a sexy thing."

Crystal took a deep breath and tried to remember the kind of sexy thing the girl had pretended to be that day.

In the washroom she took the black coat off and put it on one of the racks. How could she forget who she was?

The bra of the swimsuit fastened in front and Crystal undid it easily. The walls of the small room were mirrored and she looked at herself in them. Her breasts weren't large, but they were well shaped and stood out nicely. Loretta had said that in a year or two she would have to do exercises to keep them firm.

How could she forget who she was?

She refastened the swimsuit bra.

But Jerry was right. She was selling sex and glamour and all the things that she had, or might have, to people who believed in them.

Just forget who you are.

Crystal slipped into the white coat and returned to the set. Jerry was still on the phone. He was looking at her as he spoke. She winked at him and he winked back.

Just forget who you are, she said to herself again. There were things that were right and things that were wrong, and so many things that fell in between, gray, confusing things that nobody ever quite mentioned and that would go away if you didn't notice them.

"You look sexier already," Jerry said. "I really mean it."

"Thank you." Crystal managed a smile. "I feel sexier, too."

"Take a look at this Polaroid while I change the film." Jerry brought the picture to Crystal.

It was a nice shot. She was sitting on the chair, leaning on the table. The coat was bunched between her thighs.

"Like it?" Jerry asked.

"I like it," Crystal said.

Jerry changed the Bronica's film holder. Once he had let her shoot a few pictures of him. She had enjoyed looking down into the large screen of the camera. She remembered how self-conscious Jerry was to have his picture taken.

"Let's try a few shots in front of the city background again," Jerry said.

"Sure," Crystal said.

Jerry put the chair back in the set and handed Crystal the flower that had been in the bottle.

"Give the camera a smile," Jerry said.

Crystal turned slowly toward the camera. She smiled. She let the smile fade gradually, licking her lips slowly.

"You look sooo sexy!"

She turned. Stretched her legs, put her head down, and looked coquettishly up at the camera. She thought she might have looked silly.

"Sooo sexy!" Jerry said as the camera's motor whirred furiously.

The coat was slightly large for her and she could move, could turn her shoulders slightly, without turning the coat. The silk lining of the large coat felt cool against her bare skin.

"Pout!"

She pouted. She put her finger in her mouth.

"Good! You're great! You're simply great!"

She pulled the bottom of the coat up slowly until it was around her thighs. She had seen Rowena doing that once; she had done it herself in front of a mirror at home.

"Sensational!" he said. Jerry stopped shooting for a moment, just long enough to put a tape on the recorder. Prince's high voice came over the speakers, filling the room, the rhythm pulsating against the walls.

Crystal pretended that she was someone else, some other girl who would do anything that Jerry wanted. Almost anything.

"Move!" he said. "You're free as a bird!"

The girl fastened one button of the coat and then began to turn, her arms out, her head down and then back. Turned, spun, the hem of the coat whipping against her legs.

Jerry came closer, his face obscured behind the camera. The girl looked into it.

The girl did everything the photographer wanted. It was

almost as if she had to get into all the poses, all the sexy positions, that Crystal wouldn't.

"Sooo sexy," the photographer was saying.

The camera clicked and whirred.

"Lean back . . . don't smile, just think how beautiful you are."

The girl didn't think of how beautiful she was. In her mind she watched a photographer take pictures of another girl.

"Okay! Okay! We got it—you were wonderful!" Jerry's voice startled Crystal. He was standing near her, smiling. "You know, I think you're really a very sexy girl, but you hold it back. I think you just have to let others see it in you."

As Jerry turned away to his cameras Crystal thought of what he had said about her being really sexy. It was funny; there was a song they sang in church about letting others see you. Only in church it was "Let Others See Jesus in You."

She took the coat off and hung it up carefully. She gathered her own clothing and went into the washroom. She washed quickly and dressed even faster. For some reason she thought that Jerry might come in.

She was glad to get into her street clothes.

"Are you going back to Brooklyn, now?" Crystal saw that Jerry already had on the old army fatigue jacket he always wore.

"You wouldn't want to stop for a soda, would you?" she asked.

"I don't want to stop for anything until I get the film to the lab." Jerry tapped his camera bag. "I'll carry them over to Modernage and then start thinking about how to do a presentation for Everby."

"Oh, sure," Crystal said.

"You have cab fare home?"

"Yes."

Jerry kissed her on the forehead in the lobby. Then he hustled off into the crowd along Fifty-eighth Street.

Crystal walked slowly along Fifty-eighth until she reached Fifth Avenue. She thought of taking the "A" train to Brooklyn. She would take the "F" to West Fourth and then switch to the "A" there. It was a long ride, but she wasn't in a hurry.

8

THE ROCKING AND JERKING OF THE "A" TRAIN MADE Crystal feel uncomfortable. Across from her, two men in overalls leaned against the door. One of them winked at her and she looked away. She couldn't stop thinking about the photo session. She wished that she could have had a soda with Jerry. She wondered if he really was as high on the pictures as he seemed. She wondered, too, what the pictures were like.

The train pulled into Utica and the small woman sitting next to her got up and left. A large woman with heavy breasts that seemed to almost fall into her lap sat down quickly, her wide hips jostling Crystal slightly. Crystal looked at her and saw that her forehead was wet with perspiration. In her mind,

Crystal quickly made the woman up. A covering base, a little highlight here and there—it didn't help.

"This train go to East New York?" the woman asked in a singsong voice that sounded West Indian.

"I think so," Crystal said. She smiled.

"You a pretty little thing," the woman said.

"Thank you."

"You got to thank Jesus on your knees to be sanctified and safe from the devil's hands," the woman said. "You got to thank Him on your knees."

"Yes, ma'am."

"Lord knows I been tempted!"

"Yes, ma'am."

"But I keeps my skirts down and my eyes up to heaven."

"Yes, ma'am."

The woman nodded firmly and looked straight ahead. Crystal hoped she wasn't one of the crazy women who rode the subway.

The woman got off at the same stop as Crystal, on Fulton Street. A young girl met her at the subway. The girl looked vaguely like the woman but was very pretty. She was dark, with smooth skin and almond eyes. Crystal followed behind them for a while, listening to the lilt of their voices, watching how nicely the girl moved. The girl was older than Crystal, and Crystal wondered if she was safe from the devil's hands.

She got home and her mother was talking to Sister Gibbs. Crystal kissed her mother before slipping out of her jacket.

"How did the shooting go today?" her mother asked.

"Okay," Crystal said. "A little risqué, though."

"Loretta said we'd have full approval of any shots," Carol Brown said. "Was Jerry happy?"

"I guess."

"What you taking pictures for now?" Sister Gibbs asked.

"A magazine," Crystal answered.

"Not *Ebony*?"

"No," Crystal said, opening the door to the refrigerator. "Anything here to eat?"

"There's tuna salad," Mrs. Brown said. "It's fresh."

"How you keep your pretty little figure and eat so much, girl?" Sister Gibbs asked.

"I eat salads, mostly," Crystal answered. "And I exercise like crazy.

"What's Daddy going to eat?" Crystal spotted a cucumber in the back of the refrigerator and took it.

"Wash that thing before you eat it," her mother said.

"You ought to try to get into *Ebony*," Sister Gibbs said. "I think you can get famous in *Ebony*."

"She's been in *Ebony* and she is famous," Crystal's mother said.

"I mean really famous," Sister Gibbs said. "Where everybody know you and everything!"

"How you doing, Sister Gibbs?" Crystal sat at the table across from her. "Did I tell you that I saw Fat Pugh over on Marcy Avenue?"

"What I'm interested in him for?" Sister Gibbs shifted her ample weight in the chair. "I ain't a bit steadin' about where he is or who he be with."

"I wasn't even going to mention her," Crystal said. She was slicing the cucumber and putting the wafer-thin pieces on a saucer.

"Who?"

"I thought you weren't interested?"

"I ain't," Sister Gibbs said. "I just want to know who the hussy is. He don't go with but one old bag, anyway. That's that Dorothy Nixon from Bibleway. She ain't got no more hair than take wings and fly! Is she, Miss Brown?"

"Not much more," Crystal's mother responded to the Miss Brown.

"I think I'm going to lie down awhile," Crystal said. "I'm really pooped!"

"Who he be with, Crystal?" Sister Gibbs looked serious.

"Nobody but his sister, Jennie," Crystal said. "Every time I see him he's with her and asking about you."

"He better not be going out with nobody else and asking me to no dinner!" Sister Gibbs said. "I don't play no two-way street!"

"Pugh told Mattie's sister that he's got something to ask Sister Gibbs," Mrs. Brown said. "I think he's about ready to pop the question."

"I got to baby-sit for my cousin Evelyn tonight and I got to work tomorrow and I don't know when I'll get home," Sister Gibbs said. "I'm gonna do my hair tonight, and I wonder if you can kind of help me with my makeup, Crystal? I don't mean nothing too fancy or nothing, because I ain't trying to backslide."

"Sure," Crystal said.

"Oh, Loretta called and asked if you could make a party tomorrow night, and I said that you probably could."

"I'll have to call her," Crystal said. "I promised Pat I'd study with her."

"Perhaps we can talk about it later?"

"I guess so," Crystal said. "I think I'm going to lie down awhile."

"They working you too hard, girl," Sister Gibbs said. "That smiling in front of a camera and them hot lights will suck the juice right out of you."

Crystal went to her room and headed for the bed. She noticed a basket in the corner of the room and went to it. It was the basket her father had bought for Gizmo. The kitten was curled in one corner of the basket in a tight little ball. There was a saucer with milk in it next to the basket. Crystal knelt near the basket and rubbed her fingertips lightly through the kitten's amber fur. It moved slightly and then was still.

"Crystal?"

Crystal turned to see Sister Gibbs at the door. "Just watching Gizmo sleep."

"You all right, girl?"

"Yes, I'm fine," Crystal said.

"Your mama figured you didn't want that tuny salad so she run out to the supermarket to get you something else."

"Oh. I'm not really that hungry," Crystal said, sitting up.

"I hope you don't mind helping me with my makeup. You know, when the Good Lord was giving out looks, He must have been kind of low on His supplies when he got to me."

"I like making people up," Crystal said.

"You looking kind of down," Sister Gibbs said. "You have a rough day today?"

"The photographer wanted me to take my clothes off," Crystal said. "Nothing wrong with it, I'm just not too used to it, that's all."

"You take off *all* your clothes?"

"I was wearing a fur coat," Crystal said. "And a swimsuit, but it didn't show."

"Well, no wonder you is tired. Ain't nothing weary the body like a restless soul," Sister Gibbs said. "You gettin' into this modeling mess deeper than you want to be, huh?"

"No, it's okay." Crystal smiled. "Modeling is a business, and some things in the business you have to learn. Anyway, they're so professional, those photographers. Sometimes I think they don't even see women as people."

Sister Gibbs sat on the bed next to Crystal. She reached down and picked up the sleeping Gizmo. In her large hand the fluffy kitten looked tiny. Sister Gibbs spoke in a low voice, without turning to Crystal.

"You told your mama you posing without your clothes on?"

"Sure, she knows what modeling is like," Crystal said. "I mean, it's not like I'm doing anything wrong, Sister Gibbs."

"Uh-huh. I hear you, but you start to taking my number around with you, girl," she said. "You need you somebody to pray with you, just call me. If you find yourself in some kind of way and you can't pray, you call Sister Gibbs and we can talk till you can pray, okay?"

"Sure, Sister Gibbs." Crystal liked Sister Gibbs, but she didn't think the nut-brown woman would ever understand modeling or any other kind of modern business.

"And you just keep this one thing in mind, child," Sister Gibbs said. "It ain't knowing what's the right thing or the wrong thing that gets us into trouble. That ain't what it is. What gets us into trouble is not making up our minds about things. We goes around pretending that we don't know what to do, or we ain't thinking on it because we ain't talking about it. You get yourself into some trouble, you take a minute to make your mind up. You got the right kind of training to bring yourself through. Now you just get you some sleep and dream about something nice."

"I'll dream about making you up," Crystal said.

Sister Gibbs patted Crystal's hand, put Gizmo down, and left, hesitating at the door for a moment as if she had something else to say and then changing her mind.

"Did you ever want to be a model?" Crystal asked. "I mean, when you were my age?"

"Me?" Crystal's mother put both hands on her chest. "No, when I was a girl they didn't use as many models as they do now. There weren't as many television programs and the ones that were on had less advertising. And when they did use models they didn't use Black models.

"What I wanted to do was to sing on stage. I wanted to be in musical comedy. I was in a school production of *Oklahoma!* when I was fifteen, and it was just about the most wonderful thing that had ever happened to me. A singing coach heard me, he was Italian, and asked my parents to let me take lessons with him. When they agreed, I could have flown over

123

the city like a bird. I just could have. I studied with him for almost two years. He even got me a small part in a chorale up at Lewisohn Stadium. He talked about me studying in Europe and maybe getting into opera, because there were so few opportunities in this country. I thought I would just go from there."

"What happened?"

"I met your father, and we started going together, and before I knew it, we were married. I thought it wouldn't make a difference. He had his ideas about what we should do and I had mine. At first I was strong. I was *really* strong."

"And then?"

"And then I was pregnant," Crystal's mother said, wistfully. "But that turned out to be wonderful, too, because you were the child. Isn't that great?"

"Yeah, it's great for me," Crystal said.

"You have to be strong to do anything worthwhile, I think."

"Something funny happened at the studio today," Crystal said, not looking up from her math book. "I think Jerry really wanted me to take all my clothes off."

"He asked you to . . ." Her mother traced her fingers along the raised figures on the sides of the antique coffee set. "Of course, he didn't say anything out of line, did he?"

"No," Crystal said. "I just wanted to let you know."

"Oh, good." Carol Brown's fingers drummed nervously on her legs. "Of course, learning to pose is part of being professional. You can't think like someone who isn't in the business."

"I know," Crystal said.

"That's why you're better off not telling anyone about posing in the altogether."

"I didn't!" Crystal said. "I had a fur coat on and a swimsuit on under it."

"I didn't think you would," Carol said. "I mean, not completely nude. I just wanted you to know that if the . . . the occasion came up I would understand."

"I didn't feel very good about being 'Ooo so sexy,' either. I mean, I didn't really feel sexy."

"He didn't like the poses?"

"He liked the poses okay. I guess it was just being such a fake. It's not what I thought it would be, you know?"

"You handled it very well, apparently," Carol said. "I'm very proud of you."

"Thanks." Crystal felt somehow that they were talking about different things.

"Of course, there are people who are used to thinking professionally and people who just can't. So it's better to keep the professional matters between us. Okay?"

"Sure," Crystal said. "No problem."

"And don't forget to call Loretta about the party."

Crystal had to call three times before she got Loretta. She told her she had promised Pat that they would study together. She didn't tell her she thought that she might flunk History if they didn't study together.

"Look, why don't you see if Pat can come along, too," Loretta had said. "We can just have the limo pick her up. It might be fun for her."

Crystal called Pat and told her what Loretta had said. Pat wasn't too happy about it.

"My mother is going to go through her whole boy-crazy number," Pat said. "If I even mention boys in my house, she starts going on like I'm Madonna's bad sister or something."

"You're always asking me what it's like to be a model and go out in a limousine," Crystal said. "So come along and find out."

"What about Donald?"

"Tell him you're going to a party given by The Uniform Solution—he has to go for it. He's into music."

"I mean, can he come?"

"Pat, what are we going to do, show up with a whole bunch of sophomores at a party? I broke my neck getting you in. You really have to . . . mature."

"Okay. I'll have to tell my folks tonight. I'll let you know tomorow."

"THERE'S SOMETHING DIFFERENT ABOUT YOUR ACT, YA know what I mean?" Joe Sidney leaned across the couch to where Larry Mananero, lead guitar of The Uniform Solution, sat. "Ya got something good. It's like none of you give a crap for nothin' but you play good. Usually you see your groups that act like they don't give a crap, they don't play for crap, either."

"We're nihilists." Larry was wearing white makeup and had his hair dyed white. "We don't believe in tomorrow."

"Yeah, well, that's your problem," Sidney said, turning away. "I don't care what you believe in, so long as you got something different. You got another album in the works?"

"We're supposed to be in the studio in a month," Larry said. "A lot different than this one. It's really going to be hot."

"Yeah, maybe, maybe . . ." Sidney leaned back and started chewing on his cigar. "Look, run the music past Kelly in my office. See if he likes it. If he don't you got to come up with something new."

"That's not the point," Larry said. "If people like it or not, it doesn't make any difference in the world."

"Don't tell me what's the point, punk." Sidney pointed at Larry with his cigar. "You want to be in my production, you don't tell—you listen!"

"Yeah, man, but I don't think you understand what we're trying to do."

"It's a good thing you got a manager, because you're an idiot!" Joe Sidney stood, flicked an ash from his unlit cigar onto Larry's lap, and walked away.

"That guy is such a creep!" Larry said. "I mean, he's really a creep! One moment he's telling us how great we are, and the next he's putting us down."

"Maybe he doesn't want to use your music," Pat said.

"Oh, he'll use it," Larry said, laughing. He tossed his head back and looked at Pat. "He'll use it because it's going to make him a bundle of money!"

Pat, Crystal, and Loretta were sitting at a table near the shiny yellow Silver Cloud that the owners had made into a serving booth in the Kaliber Club. The club had been closed to the public for the private party. Crystal hadn't recognized many of the guests. They were, for the most part, record-company people. Sidney's company was listed as co-producer with Polar Productions, and he and several executives from Polar had been introduced before the party swung into high gear.

"I'm not trying to put off the guy, Crystal," Larry said. "But what Sidney sees is flesh and money. He wants his pound either way."

Pat glanced at Crystal and Loretta.

"Well, Crystal will make him a lot of money, too," Loretta said. "And that's why he's anxious to use her in his upcoming production."

"She'll be fabulous!" Larry answered. "And I know it's going to make money. I mean, *Flashdance* was a lousy story, the characters weren't believable, but it clicked because the music was right and the flesh was beautiful."

"I liked the story," Pat said.

"You liked the story?" Larry took Pat's hand. "You are so beautiful and so innocent. Will you marry me?"

"You're crazy!" Pat laughed and retrieved her hand.

"Does that mean yes?"

"No, it doesn't," Pat said.

"Oh, marry him!" Crystal teased.

"You want to just fool around?" Larry put his head on Pat's shoulder.

"I don't think so," Pat said, seriously.

"We'll see," Larry said. Then he turned to Crystal. "Did Panting Sidney, that's what we call him, make a grab for you yet?"

"Not yet," Crystal said. "Fortunately."

Larry saw one of the members of The Uniform Solution headed toward the stage. "I've got to get up on stage. We promised to play a medley-type thing before the party ends."

Pat and Crystal watched as Larry made his way through the noisy crowd toward the small stage that had been set up for the occasion.

They watched him stop and talk to several of the guests, greeting each one with exaggerated movements, getting slightly wilder as he got ready to play.

"I think he's on something," Crystal said.

"You think that guy Sidney is actually going to make a move on you?" Pat asked.

"Probably," Crystal said.

"Being moved on is part of the business," Loretta said. "Lying down for it isn't."

"You ought to slap his face if he even tries!" Pat said.

"Pat, grow up!"

"Why should you have to put up with his nasty ways?" Pat said. "If some creep like that came up and started making a move on me, I'd tell him off!"

"Don't worry," Crystal snapped. "Nobody's going to ask you!"

"I didn't say . . ." Pat put her hands in her lap. "I just meant that you shouldn't let people push you around."

"Everybody's not as uptight as you are," Crystal said. "Let's just leave it at that."

"I'm not uptight, Crissie," Pat said.

Crystal got up and looked around the floor. Dave Lenz, the drummer from The Uniform Solution, was in the middle of the floor, dancing by himself. Crystal got up and walked over to him.

"You always dance by yourself?" she asked. "And how come you're not playing with the band?"

"Just waiting for you to dance with, love," he said. "And they're not really playing. They're just synching the sound-track."

Crystal began to dance. She was a good dancer and she knew it. The music was, like all of The Uniform Solution's music, almost otherworldly. Crystal moved to it easily, giving herself over to the steady rhythm that acted as a counterpoint to the wandering tune.

There were people watching as Crystal and Dave danced slowly in the middle of the room. A few of the other dancers stopped to see what they were doing. Dave was wearing a powder blue base and had his hair dyed the same color. Someone dimmed the lights and put a spot on Dave and Crystal.

Crystal gave herself to the music and put all of her body into what she was doing. She thought of herself as beautiful. She thought of herself as sexy. Everyone was watching her. It was a good feeling. She knew that Pat would be watching. Pat, with her shocked face. So let her be shocked, Crystal thought. Maybe a little shock would make her less sure of herself.

Crystal put her hands on the outside of her thighs and slid her skirt up. She moved closer and closer to Dave until, when she rotated her hips slowly forward, they would almost touch him. Someone, probably Larry, began playing a wild guitar solo over the record. The lights were getting dimmer. Just before they went out completely Crystal dug her teeth lightly into Dave's chest.

"To tell you the truth, I didn't expect it of her." Loretta was putting on her coat to leave. "She's usually so demure."

"She's wild, I like that," Joe Sidney said. "That dance she did with the drummer was a real hot number. We got to use that in the movie."

"So you want to sign her now?" Loretta offered Sidney a pen.

"We'll sign her to a commitment sheet," Sidney said.

"I don't want a commitment sheet, because she's not important enough to make a difference," Loretta said. "If she's in the movie, then it's fine; if she's not, the commitment sheet won't help a bit. You said you like her—why don't you sign her?"

"What am I gonna do if somebody puts up the money to back somebody else, huh? What am I gonna do then?" Sidney said. "Suppose somebody puts up a couple of million to back this little girl here. What's your name, honey?"

"Pat."

"Then what am I going to do?" Sidney asked.

"Pat's not even in the business, she's just a friend of Crystal's," Loretta said. "And anyway, where's your artistic integrity?"

"I lost it a while back." Sidney looked out over the dance floor. "There's a lot of people here tonight, and she got her picture taken more than anybody."

"When do you expect the finances to clear?" Loretta asked.

"Next week," Sidney said. "I see the money people Monday. If they say I can go with her I'll go with her. Where does she live?"

"Brooklyn."

"Good. We can use that in the publicity," Sidney said. "'Brooklyn slum girl makes good.' I'll get Larry to give her a lift home tonight."

"Why?" Loretta asked.

"I got to see how she and Larry get along," Sidney said. "If the money guys don't go for the angle I gave him in the treatment, then maybe I can switch the whole thing to her and Larry. Instead of her dancing with the drummer, she can dance with Larry. Yeah, they can have a real hot number together. That way if the rushes look like garbage, I can still have something by switching the end around and going for the teenybopper market."

"That's a hotter market, anyway," Loretta said. "It might be easier to get the money for that market."

"Yeah, well, I'll go whichever way the money comes," Sidney said. "You know what I mean?"

"You mean your creative talents are flexible," Loretta said, glancing at Pat.

"Whatever," Sidney responded.

"I can't wait!" Pat said. "It's one o'clock already. My mom is going to kill me!"

"She's not going to kill you," Crystal said. "If she's awake and looking out of the window, she's going to see you pull up in the limo and she's not going to say a thing. If you look like you're really making it, people don't care what you do."

"She's going to kill me," Pat said.

"Why are you trying to ruin my evening?" Crystal asked.

"Crissie, I'm not trying to ruin anything."

"Then just go along with it." Crystal put her arm around Pat's shoulders. "How wrong can it be if we're together? Right?"

"Right." Pat forced a smile.

"And don't start sniffling, okay? They want Larry to take me home in the limo because that kind of thing is good for my career. Don't blow it for me, Pat. Just try to be cool."

Larry popped the cork on the champagne just as the stretch limo pulled away from the curb. The seats in the back of the limo were in an oval around the small bar.

"We ought to drink this from somebody's shoes, but I think everybody except Dave is wearing open toes tonight," Larry said. He poured champagne for the four of them.

Crystal snuggled up to Larry and put her head on his chest.

"I think she's trying to convert me in midstream," Larry said, pulling Crystal closer.

"I wonder if her friend would like to convert me on the way to Brooklyn?" Dave said.

"Pat's a little tense," Crystal said.

"I'm not tense," Pat said.

"Good," Larry said. "Let's see a conversion."

Dave pulled Pat to him and started to kiss her. At first she started to push him away, and then she allowed him to kiss her. When Crystal saw that Pat was coming up for air, she turned to Larry and kissed him.

Larry poured some more champagne for himself. Car lights flashed by them, making his pale, made-up face look weird in the darkened limousine.

Dave was fumbling with the front of Pat's dress.

Crystal told herself that Pat would do what she wanted to do. She was only four months younger than Crystal. Larry had his arm around Crystal's shoulders and was holding her gently. Crystal looked up at him and saw that he was watching Dave and Pat intently.

Crystal couldn't see very well what was happening in the dim light. She caught glimpses of Dave and Pat and thought she saw Pat trying to push his hands away. She knew Dave had been drinking too much. For a moment, as they passed a sign on Broadway, Crystal found herself looking into Pat's eyes. There was a sadness in them, a sadness that lasted for a long second, then disappeared as the interior of the car went dark.

The yellow light on the stairwell at 360 Putnam Avenue made the dingy walls look yellow. They hadn't spoken for nearly ten minutes. Pat leaned against the wall, crying softly.

"I don't know what to do," she said. "I just don't know what to do."

"Why do you have to do anything?" Crystal said. "You just go in the house and say that you're tired and you'll tell everybody what a wonderful time you had in the morning."

"I just feel so dirty."

"You didn't go all the way, or anything like that, so you don't have anything to worry about!" Crystal said. "I don't know why you're so upset."

"Why don't you say something nice to me!" Pat said. "I thought you were my friend."

"I'm here, aren't I?" Crystal said. "I've got to walk to Gates Avenue by myself now."

"I just feel so terrible!"

"*Why?* I really want to know why?"

"I don't know," Pat said softly. "Because I don't feel good about myself, I guess. I always thought I was so special. Then here I am kissing a guy and letting him put his hands all over me in the back of a car."

"It's not that big a deal, Pat," Crystal said. "You have to ask yourself what you did wrong. If you don't come up with something, something real, then it's okay."

"Do you really believe that?"

"Sometimes," Crystal said.

"You're not going to tell anybody, are you?" Pat asked. Her voice was soft and it made Crystal sad to hear her.

"Of course not," Crystal said. She pulled Pat to her feet and put her arms around her.

When Crystal got home, her father was sleeping at the kitchen table. He was in his undershirt. She figured he had been waiting up for her. She looked at the clock over the sink. It was almost three. She went quietly into her room, undressed in the dark, and slipped into bed.

She couldn't sleep. She kept thinking about Pat. She wondered what Pat would think about the pictures she had posed for. She had thought about telling her. After what had happened in the limousine, even though Pat hadn't really done anything terrible, Crystal knew that she would have an easier time talking to her friend. Maybe they could even be better friends now than before.

She heard footsteps. It had to be her father. She closed her eyes and pretended to be asleep as the door opened.

"Crystal?" The light switched on.

Crystal kept her eyes shut even when her father kissed her goodnight.

10

CRYSTAL HAD BEEN STUDYING GEOMETRY SINCE EARLY Tuesday morning. Mrs. O'Donnell had announced a test at the end of class the day before.

"Anybody absent tomorrow will have to take a much harder make-up test," the teacher had announced. "And let me warn you, the test will be at least fifty percent of your grade for the quarter. Any questions?"

Crystal wanted to study with Pat but hadn't called her. Pat had been quiet in church Sunday and had refused her invitation to come up to Crystal's house for lunch. In school, Monday, she had been all right but still a little distant.

"You still thinking about the other night?" Crystal had asked her on the bus.

"A little," Pat said. "You know what I did?"

"What?"

"Went out and bought their album," Pat said. "The old one, *Noises in a Swound*. What a creepy name."

"What are you doing tonight?"

"Some things for my mother," Pat had said. "Paying bills, that kind of thing."

"Oh."

Crystal had wanted to say more, to talk about how Pat felt, but she didn't. She especially wanted to know why Pat had bought the album. Crystal thought that if Pat had really felt bad about kissing Dave in the car and letting him put his hands on her, she wouldn't even want to think about it. Instead, she had bought The Uniform Solution's album, even though Crystal knew that Pat didn't like their music that much.

The studying didn't help very much. She hadn't noticed herself falling behind in math. The test was on Tuesday afternoon, and she had promised Loretta she would work with Jerry the next day on a new portfolio. By the time the shooting was to start she was glad to stop thinking about math.

"Just relax, Erika," Loretta was saying to the new girl that Jerry was testing. "Try whatever poses you want and let the photographer do the rest."

"Okay," Jerry said.

Loretta was standing just to the side of Crystal, out of camera range, as Jerry started shooting the nervous girl.

"Okay, lean a little forward in the chair and try to give me the expressions I ask for," Jerry said.

"Don't worry if they don't come out right," Loretta said. "We won't have the pictures captioned, so they won't know what you're trying for."

"Be happy!" Jerry said.

The girl tried to look happy but was clearly too nervous.

"Just relax," Jerry said. "Move around."

Alyce Winslow leaned aginst the wall, her head to the side. Crystal saw Alyce's face change ever so slightly as Jerry gave the commands to Erika. What Erika struggled for, Alyce did without thinking. She was good.

Erika was tall and elegant with wide blue eyes and good bones. Her nose and mouth were attractive also, but her posture was bad. She was very round-shouldered. She was lovely, Crystal thought, but definitely not a model. Crystal looked at Loretta, who, in turn, shrugged.

A few more awkward attempts at conveying happiness brought the young girl close to tears. Then she smiled and Crystal turned just in time to see Alyce pull her face into a comical pose.

As Erika was putting her things in her bag Loretta told her that she couldn't handle her booking. The girl nodded curtly, pushed the last of her things into her bag, and left as quickly as possible.

"Alyce, you're no help at all," Loretta said, smiling.

"Oh, I thought I was trooly, trooly wonnerful," Alyce

said, pursing her lips into a small red bow.

"She ought to be a comedian instead of a model," Rowena said. "She's really good at it."

"You still want the proofs?" Jerry asked.

"Let's just go straight to glossies," Loretta said, going through her purse. "She's a friend of a friend. So many people think because a girl is pretty she can model. Anybody got a token?"

"Jerry has a little drawer full of tokens," Rowena said.

Loretta gave Jerry a look as Rowena went into the next room to get the tokens.

"Jerry, you said you would let me take some pictures," Alyce said. "Why don't you set the camera up and I'll take a roll of Crystal before she leaves. Okay, Crystal?"

"Okay," Crystal said.

"You need one or two?" Rowena asked, returning with the tokens.

"One's fine," Loretta said. "Crystal, I'll call you in a day or two. Meanwhile, get more sleep and give yourself a facial, you look a little dry around the eyes."

"Yes, boss lady!" Crystal grinned broadly.

"Everybody's a clown today!" Loretta said. "Time for me to leave."

"Alyce, the camera is set up, let's see what you're going to do."

"Oh, no," Alyce said. "I want everybody out, so my creativity won't be stifled."

"Do you know which button to push to take a picture?" Jerry asked.

"Yes, dah-ling."

Jerry and Rowena left the studio with Loretta. Alyce went to where Crystal still sat on the stool and lifted Crystal's chin up slightly.

"You look official," Crystal said.

"I think I'd like to do photography one day," Alyce said. "Perhaps when I'm old I can have a studio."

"Were you working today?"

"Loretta had me doing a cat commercial," Alyce said. "They had this other girl there—I think she was from Harlan-Stone or some other stupid agency. Anyway, she's about nine, and she doesn't have any boobs, but she's trying to be sexy. She's supposed to bring me the kitten and say, in this little cute voice, how she loves the kitten and do I think the kitten loves her."

"She's doing a midget bit?"

"Right." Alyce was looking into the camera. "She's supposed to be about five and she *looks* about five, but she thinks, if we can use that word, that she's about seventeen and hot stuff. So it took us four hours to shoot a commercial that should have taken us fifteen minutes."

"And the director let it go?"

"I think he's sleeping with the tot's mom or something," Alyce said. "Smile."

Crystal smiled. The camera clicked and the motor whirred as the film was automatically advanced.

"You're very beautiful," Alyce said.

"Thank you," Crystal said. "So are you."

"I think Rowena's a hag." Alyce looked up from the viewer.

"Could you turn your head a little to the left?"

"I think she's okay," Crystal said. She turned her head. The camera clicked.

"I saw the pictures Jerry took of you," Alyce said. "They're really special."

"Oh? He didn't mention them to me."

"Rowena took the finals over to Everby," Alyce said. "Or at least that's what she said. I just saw the proofs when I was looking for shots of me. I have this one picture in my portfolio I thought was just great, now I hate it. That ever happen to you?"

"Sometimes."

"Look into the camera and smile, but try not to show your teeth, because too much of your gum shows when you smile," Alyce said.

"Jerry doesn't think so," Crystal said, defensively.

"I see he had you posing in fur," Alyce said. "I thought they were saving you for the wholesome stuff. Turn to the right."

Crystal caught her breath.

"You're not smiling, dear," Alyce said. "I mean if you want to do that kind of posing it's okay with me."

"If you have a nice body," Crystal said, trying to regain her composure, "you can show it off. If you develop a little, you can show more of yourself, too. And anyway, the pictures weren't nudies or anything."

"They aren't exactly classy, either," Alyce said. "But of course you knew that, didn't you? Smile."

"You're just jealous," Crystal said.

"The one with that cute little pout. Everby can put that on the wall of his penthouse."

"Where did you say you saw the pictures?" Crystal asked.

Alyce glanced toward the door, then went to the file cabinet. She opened one of the sliding drawers and took out some pictures.

Crystal came over and looked at the pictures as Alyce laid them out, one by one, on the top of the cabinet. Crystal had to look at them closely to make sure they were really of her.

"They're really something," Alyce said. "And the ones *La Femme* doesn't use, you can always save for *Grind*."

"Isn't that where your mother got her start?" Crystal asked, walking away from the pictures.

"I really have to go now," Alyce said, turning away. "I'm working this afternoon on another *boring* cat food commercial."

"Do you get to eat out of a bowl?" Crystal asked as Alyce left.

When Alyce had gone, Crystal went back to the pictures and looked at them. They made her look as sexy as Jerry said she was. One of them, with the coat open more than the others, made her look as if she were nude under the coat. Jerry must have airbrushed the swimsuit out!

They seemed to be more than pictures. They seemed to have a life of their own. The tears came stinging to her eyes.

"Hey, what are you doing?" It was Rowena.

"Looking at the pictures Jerry took," Crystal said.

"I think they're great!" Rowena said.

"Did he show them to . . . anyone?"

"He just sent a set over to *La Femme*," Rowena said.

"They're terrible!"

"Crystal, they're not. They're a little sexy, but they're not that bad."

"Then why does it seem like . . ."

"Hey, Crystal, it's cool." Rowena put her arm around Crystal. "It really is. I took some pictures once that were a lot worse than these. Jerry's got a set."

"Jerry took them?"

"Yeah, that's why it's cool," Rowena said. "Jerry and I are tight, and we respect each other. But they all take them. Jerry says that some photographers sell them privately. But they'll never get shown. Jerry wouldn't do anything like that. He's real cool. Honest."

"Can I see your pictures?"

Rowena looked at Crystal. Her face moved, almost as if she were trying to smile but couldn't. "Sure."

Rowena went to the side of the file cabinet and took some keys that were on a hook. She opened a drawer and took out a small leather portfolio. She put it on the desk in front of Crystal.

Crystal opened the portfolio. Rowena was posing in high boots with her hands on her hips. The black-and-white photos made her skin look whiter. The low angle made her forehead higher, too. She looked tougher than Crystal knew her to be.

"I think they're dynamite," Rowena was saying. "They make me look like a real actress. I'm being, like, dominant with that wardrobe, right?"

"When did you take these?" Crystal asked. She turned to a

picture of Rowena with her leg over the back of a chair.

"About six months ago. I had just lost the perfume account and I needed to do some work. This was different; it took me out of my mood. I think they're really dynamite."

"Who was the client?" Crystal looked at Rowena. The older girl kept her eyes on the pictures.

"I don't remember," Rowena said. "It was a job."

"You want to go to Manhattan with me?" Crystal asked, abruptly.

"Manhattan? You want me to?"

"I don't think I can deal with school today."

"You want to get made up?"

"For what?"

"We can just do it for kicks," Rowena said. "We can make each other up like crazy, you know, a little far out. Then we'll go into Manhattan, and everybody will look at us and try to figure out who we are. I like that."

"Why?"

"Because then I can be anybody I want to be. I just don't have to be me."

"Is just being you that bad?"

"Sometimes it is." Rowena shrugged. "You want to?"

"Sure."

Crystal made up Rowena first. She brushed on eyeliner because she was too nervous to use a pencil and then started putting on mascara. "Why do you think we'll be better friends because we have pictures?" she asked.

"Because we know more about each other," Rowena said. "If you only get to look at a person one way, you only get to know them one way."

144

"The pictures aren't real," Crystal said. She put beige lipstick on Rowena with a slightly lighter liner.

"How do I look?"

"One minute." Crystal added highlighter along Rowena's nose. "There, you're beautiful."

Rowena looked in the mirror and liked what she saw. "You're good," she said. "I look better like this than when Franke or somebody like that makes me up. Especially with the eyes, the way you've done them. But I'm not special like this. I'm not pretty enough to be just me, you know what I mean?"

"Yes, you are," Crystal said.

"Sit down," Rowena said. "I'll show you what pretty is."

She put a mixture of liquid pink and beige foundation on Crystal.

"You've got really nice skin," she said. "I'm not putting any contour on your cheeks. I like them a little round. That makes you look young and that's good. Alyce has an old face. She's younger than both of us, but she could be thirty if she wanted. Especially if she uses a lot of shadow over her eyes."

"I don't like her at all," Crystal said.

"Alyce? She's okay," Rowena said. "She can't be a friend or anything like that, but she's okay. She just doesn't know about hurting people yet."

"You like her?"

"I think she's okay. You don't have to like me to get me to like you," Rowena said. "I like a lot of people who don't like me."

She finished doing Crystal's face, stepped back, and gave her friend the thumbs-up sign.

"We ready?" Crystal asked.

"Let's get into the city and do it."

Rowena had money, and they took a cab from Brooklyn to Manhattan. The cab driver asked if they were models, and Rowena said no, that they were in films.

"Oh, have I seen any of your movies?" the driver asked, looking into his rearview mirror.

"Mostly we've been doing things in Italy," Rowena said.

"And now you're going to be making movies in this country?"

"How did you *know*?" Crystal put on her shocked look.

"Look, we get lots of people in these cabs," the driver said. "You pick up little things here, little things there. After a while you begin to know a lot. We'd be the best spies in the world."

"Well, we hope you keep this to yourself," Rowena said, nudging Crystal with her elbow as the cab pulled up outside of Bergdorf's.

"Of course," the driver said. "And what did you say your names were again?"

"Elizabeth Harmon," Crystal said. "And of course, this is Vadrika."

"Yeah, of course." The driver nodded. He offered them the change for the twenty, but they were already walking down Fifth Avenue.

They went into almost every store from Fifty-seventh to the French Building on Forty-fifth on the east side of Fifth Avenue, then crossed and did the same coming up Fifth on the west side of New York's most glamorous thoroughfare. They didn't buy anything, but Rowena kept asking the salesclerks if they would have the things she looked at until that weekend.

"You going to buy that stuff this weekend?" Crystal asked.

"No," Rowena said. "But they don't know that."

They bought hot dogs from a vendor near Doubleday's and ate them in front of a construction site. The construction workers, mostly young men with hard, flat bellies, whistled and called to them. Older men, with bellies that hung over their belts, looked on.

"This is what I like to do," Rowena said.

"Turn on all the guys and then walk away?" Crystal asked.

"Walk away with a friend," Rowena said.

They walked a little way down Fifty-seventh, looking and being looked at. "I hate the pictures," Crystal said, suddenly.

"It's okay," Rowena said. "We've got each other. You and me and Alyce. Right?"

"Right!" Crystal said, taking Rowena's arm.

"Yo, mama!" A tall, skinny messenger, wearing tight, black biking pants over a gray sweat suit, stopped his bike in front of Crystal and Rowena as they made their way through traffic across Fifty-seventh street. "Y'all look good enough to eat!"

Rowena and Crystal looked straight ahead.

"I know I'm disgusting to you pretty ladies," the messenger called after them. "But what you want from a high school dropout?"

They walked for another hour, stopping on the corners long enough to attract attention, occasionally stopping in front of store windows so that passersby could notice their reflections, stopping in Rizzoli's so that a middle-aged Black clerk could show them outrageously priced prints.

The weather grew cooler. They talked less. They struck fewer casual poses. They grew tired. After a while, as the evening rush hour began, they were hardly noticed.

"I just think I need a vacation, that's all!" Crystal pushed a piece of cubed cantaloupe around the edge of her plate. "Anyway, my grades are really falling. I'm just so far behind in everything."

"What are you *talking* about?" Carol Brown leaned against the refrigerator. "What are you *talking* about? We've worked so hard for this, and now you just want to give it up?"

"I can still be a model. I just want to rest for a while," Crystal protested.

"*Rest?* Now that you're on top of things? This is the opportunity you've been waiting for!"

"I don't like what I'm doing. I don't like the pictures I'm in, I don't like the people, I don't like the magazines . . ."

"Crystal, please, don't start whining!"

"I'm not— Mom, what's so important about this, anyway?"

"It's important not to throw away your chance when it's in your lap!" The vein in Carol's neck bulged as she spoke.

"The chance to have my picture taken for a dirty old man?"

"Grow up!" her mother screamed. "You have the chance to live as well as you please, to take what you want from life instead of standing on the sidelines, hoping a few crumbs fall your way. I know what it's like waiting for the crumbs. I've been waiting for them for the last fifteen years!"

"Mama, don't say that!"

"Why not? Every day I have to walk around the garbage in the streets to get to our building. Every day I hold my breath so I don't have to smell everybody's life as I pass through these hallways. Every day I dream of what life could have, should have, would have been if I had known anything. *Anything!*"

"I don't want to throw anything away," Crystal said. "I just thought . . . you said I didn't have to do the modeling if I wasn't happy with it."

"Oh, Crystal, baby, you're right." Carol Brown slumped into a chair. "That's what I said. And you don't have to. You don't, really. Sometimes I just get to thinking about what life is about, what it's really about, and I look around here and I just don't think this is it. I want so much for you, baby."

"I know, Mama. Let me think about it."

"No, if you don't want it anymore, you should call Loretta. She's been good to us and we should lay it on the line to her."

"Does the money change things?" Crystal asked. "I know I'm making a lot of money."

"You're what's important, Crystal," Carol said. "Now, go get dressed for school. Maybe . . . maybe, you can just bring that grade up to a B-plus."

"Sure."

Crystal went to her room and put on a dark-red pleated skirt and a sweater. She hated to hurt her mother, but it was true, she was tired. At first modeling had just been glamorous and exciting, but now she felt tired all the time.

Gizmo was under the bed, as usual. She took him out and put him on the bed. He pranced around slowly, then stopped and stretched and began to scratch at the bedspread.

"Don't!" Crystal admonished softly.

The kitten looked at her with wide eyes, his tail straight up. She'd have to teach him to behave, she thought. She gave him a little push and watched him fall over. He didn't care about falling, he didn't know anything about being hurt.

"Get up, silly!" she said.

Gizmo lay on his back and looked at her.

"You want to hear the poem I wrote about you for school?" Crystal asked, teasing Gizmo with her finger.

She went to her drawer and got the binder the poem was in.

"It's got to be the best poem ever written to a kitten for our school magazine," Crystal said. "So you be very good and listen carefully."

She read the poem to Gizmo, holding the paper inches above him as he, still lying on his back, tried to reach it with his claws:

> "To My Kitten, Gizmo
> by Crystal Brown
>
> You're very beautiful, you know,
> Eyes of amber set aglow,
> A look so fierce, and yet so mild.
> There is a beast in you, and there is a child,
> And yet, you're very beautiful, you know.
> I watch you stalk some shadowed prey.
> Is it real or do you play?
> Are you truly what you seem?
> Are you the dreamer, or the dream?
> Eyes of amber set aglow,
> You are quite beautiful, you know."

150

She put the kitten back on the floor. She knew her mother was disappointed in her. It would be easier telling Loretta. Loretta would say something about her throwing away an opportunity, but she wouldn't push it. That wasn't Loretta's way.

The crash of glass brought Crystal abruptly to a sitting position. She listened as the noises came from the kitchen. There were crashes, the sounds of things being broken, and most terribly, the small whimpering sounds in between.

"Mama!" Crystal raced to the kitchen and grabbed the doorway for support. There, nearly flat against the patterned wallpaper, her mother slid along the wall, banging her fists into the gay patterns. And there were the sounds. Quiet, almost soft sounds of anger and frustration.

"Mama!" Crystal went to her mother as quickly as possible. She put her arms around the older woman's shoulders as the woman huddled away from her in a corner. "Mama . . . Mama . . . please!"

Carol Brown, still facing away from Crystal, straightened up.

"Mama . . ."

"I just feel so frustrated. . . ." Crystal could hardly hear her mother's words. "And I don't have the right . . . I just don't have the right!"

"Mama! Mama!" Crystal was crying.

"I'm okay." Carol turned and wiped at her face with her hands.

"Mama, please don't cry . . . Please be all right . . ."

"I'm okay, now." Her mother shook her head from side to

side. She took her daughter's hand and held it against her cheek. "I'll clean this up."

"No, I'll do it later," Crystal said. "It won't take me long. Why don't you lie down for a while?"

They half walked, half stumbled into her mother's bedroom. Carol Brown fell across the bed and was still. Crystal sat by her side, the tears streaming down her face, her lips twisted in the agony of the pain she felt.

"Mama . . . oh, Mama . . ."

"Honey, will you do something for me? Please?"

"Anything, Mama," Crystal said. "Anything."

"Please don't tell your father about this," Carol said. "It was so silly for me to lose control of myself. Your father's got enough worries on him about money and keeping the family together. Please don't tell him, honey."

"I won't tell him, Mama."

The phone rang.

"Let it ring," Crystal said.

"Life has to go on," her mother said. "No matter what I feel."

Carol picked up the telephone.

"Your mother called," Loretta said. "What's up?"

Crystal looked at her mother. "It's Loretta."

"I called her to tell her that you were . . ." She turned away.

"Hello, Loretta?" Crystal's hand trembled as she held the phone. "Mom just wondered if I would be working this weekend?"

Loretta said she wouldn't be working that weekend. Crystal hung up the phone and turned to her mother. The woman who she had thought just the day before could have been a model now looked old, drawn. Crystal knelt on the floor beside Carol Brown.

"Mom, are you going to be okay?" Crystal asked.

"I will be," she said. "If you're okay, then so am I, honey."

Her mother smiled and kissed Crystal on the cheek.

Crystal pulled the sheet around her mother's shoulders and went into the kitchen. The damage wasn't that bad. Only a few of the cheaper glasses had been broken. Crystal swept up the broken fragments of glass and then wiped a coffee stain from the wall. When she looked back into the bedroom, her mother's eyes were closed.

Usually she didn't make up to go to school, but she stood in front of the mirror putting on the darker-than-usual foundation. She knew it would at least help cover the anguish she felt.

She felt so alone. You have to grow up, she said to herself. You have to know what it's all about.

And what was it all about? It was having people you love depend on you. Helping her parents, who wanted so much for her. Not letting people down.

Crystal was surprised at how she looked. For some reason she had taken the eyebrow pencil and drawn huge black circles around her eyes. She hadn't even been aware of doing it. She looked horrible. She quickly sponged it off and started over. Her hands were shaking. She knew it would be difficult to look good.

"So anyway, it came down to either a fashion show," Pat said, "a beauty pageant, or a volleyball marathon."

"How can you raise money playing volleyball?" Crystal asked.

"You get sponsors," Donald said. "For every point that's scored, the sponsor gives a penny. So if we play volleyball all night long and the score ends up like two hundred to one hundred and fifty, something like that, then each sponsor has to shell out three dollars and fifty cents."

"And everybody liked that?"

"Nobody liked that," Pat said. She carefully wiped the top of the can of Diet Coke she had bought. "But everybody figured that if we had a beauty pageant you would win, and nobody wanted to be in a fashion show if you were in it, because they couldn't compete with you."

"Which is true," Donald said, pleased with himself.

"Are you telling me, Mr. Evans, that *I* cannot compete with Crissie?"

"No, I'm just saying what everybody else is saying," Donald answered quickly.

"And what are you saying, Mr. Evans?" Crystal asked, taking Donald by his tie.

"Roses are red, violets are blue, if you ask me who's the prettiest, I got to name two!"

"You think he's copping out, Crissie?" Pat asked.

"He just might be, but I think we'll let him slide this time."

"Where were you during the meeting?" Pat asked.

"I had to give Mr. Dennison this poem I wrote for the school magazine."

"Is he going to publish it?"

"I don't think so," Crystal said. The day had hardly begun and she was already exhausted. "But I did it anyway."

"Hey, my group is rehearsing this afternoon in the music room," Donald said. "If you ladies want to come by and hear some fresh sounds, you're welcome."

"Maybe some other time," Pat said, lifting her shoulder in a mock sexy pose. "We wouldn't want to distract you boys."

Donald went to his French class, and Pat asked Crystal what she thought of him.

"I like him," Crystal answered. "You must be falling in love, or you wouldn't ask so much."

"I like him a lot," Pat said. "You looked upset when you got here this morning. You okay?"

"My mom was sick," Crystal said. "She was feeling better by the time I left."

"Anything serious?"

"I don't know," Crystal said. "I guess I don't want to talk about it."

"Crissie, are we sort of . . . you know . . . drifting apart?" Pat asked. "Because I'm over what happened before. It was just the little girl in me coming out. That's why I was upset. Afterwards, I thought about it a lot. I figured if you were going to fool around a little, that was the best way to do it. You know, in a limo and all."

"Why would you say something like that? Why?" Crystal felt a sudden surge of anger as she turned toward her friend. "Why?"

"Cris . . ?" Pat saw the rage in Crystal's face and took a

step backward. Crystal got up quickly and walked away. She was mad—she didn't know why, but she was mad and even hurt. She stopped in the hallway and leaned against the wall until she got herself together again, then tried to put it all out of her mind as she started toward her next class.

It was on the way to English that Crystal ran into Jim Dennison. He asked if she had a moment to discuss the poem she had given him. She said that she was in a hurry and that she would see him in the magazine office after school. She knew, even then, that she wouldn't.

11

"THE ROGER HALLEN SHOW?" DANIEL BROWN WAS IN his shirtsleeves at the kitchen table. His dark, muscular arms were folded across his chest. "She going to sing or something?"

"No, she's going to talk about what it's like being one of the most exciting young models in America." Loretta Barrett stirred her coffee by moving the spoon quickly at the top of the cup. "I'm sure he'll ask her how she manages to balance her schoolwork with her modeling, that kind of thing. It'll be wonderful for her."

"And how much she get for being on his show?" Crystal's father asked.

"Five hundred dollars," Crystal said. "How do I look?"

"That's all?" Daniel turned his head sideways.

"What they pay is the absolute minimum they can get away with," Loretta said. "The prestige is supposed to be payment enough."

"Do you really have to work tonight, Daddy?" Crystal asked. "You could come see me."

"You got to be kidding." Daniel smiled. "I'm going on in to work at the hospital the way I usually do. I'm going to sit there on the third floor where the color television is, and when the Roger Hallen Show comes on and my baby shows up and the guys turn to me and say, 'Hey, man, ain't that your daughter?' you know what I'm gonna say? I'm gonna look real close like I ain't sure, and then I'm gonna say something like 'Yeah, that's her' and make believe I'm reading a newspaper or something."

"Get out of here, Daddy," Crystal said.

"Ain't no 'get out of here,'" Daniel Brown said. "When Timmy's kid got a scholarship to Fordham, and it was in the newspaper, do you know what he did?"

"He bought a copy for everybody," Loretta guessed.

"A copy?" Daniel looked at Loretta. "He bought *two* copies, one for us to read and one for us to save!"

"We'd better get going," Carol said. "Crystal you look beautiful."

"She always looks beautiful," Daniel said. "I told you beauty was in my genes."

Loretta, Carol, and Crystal left. Daniel waited until he thought they were downstairs and then went to the front window and peeked out the curtains as they got into the waiting limousine.

Crystal watched Roger Hallen on the monitor behind the curtain. The makeup girl stood near her, sponge in hand. As Hallen ended the thirty-second spot for United Airlines the assistant director pointed toward Crystal and the makeup girl quickly touched the sponge to her upper lip to remove any traces of moisture.

"You're beautiful," she whispered.

The director held up four fingers as Hallen's voice came over the monitor.

"You see these beautiful girls on magazine covers, you see them on television; if you're lucky you see them dashing around the fashion centers of the city. Tonight, we have a very beautiful, very charming young lady who's making quite a name for herself—Miss Crystal Brown. . . ."

The stagehand held the curtain for Crystal as the audience began to applaud. Roger Hallen stood as she went to the large desk he sat behind. He was shorter than she thought he would be, and she was more nervous than she thought she would be. Loretta had warned her that the chair next to Hallen's desk would be uncomfortable. It was, the seat being slanted slightly forward.

"So, how's the modeling business?" Hallen asked as Crystal sat next to his desk.

"Just fine," Crystal said. A man with headphones, out of camera range, was holding up a picture of a can of dog food.

"I understand that besides being a model, you've written a book?" Hallen said, twisting a pencil between his fingers.

"A book?" Crystal shook her head. "No."

"Oh, that's right," Hallen corrected himself. "I'm sorry, I

got my notes wrong, you're *planning* to write a book. Let's sneak in a quick word from one of the sponsors, and then we'll talk more about your modeling *and* the book."

The offstage monitor showed a close-up of Roger Hallen's face as the director gave hand signals. A screen at the side of the camera Hallen was looking at lit up and a message began to roll slowly. Hallen read it in a way that looked as if he were making it up as he went along.

"Dogs are man's best friends, we've said that time and time again and I guess we've actually become dogs' best friends, too. I think the makers of Gro-Chow had this in mind when they created their new line of nutritionally balanced dog food."

The red light on the camera went out, and a taped commercial began to play on the monitor. The director came over to the desk in response to Hallen's beckoning.

"I thought she wrote a book," Hallen said, nodding toward Crystal. He pulled a book from a table behind his desk.

"The next guest wrote the book, a thing on the changing values of family life," the director said with a shrug.

"Look, tell her the show's running behind schedule or something." Hallen handed the book to the director.

"Fine." The director took the book, tossed it to an assistant, and ran his finger across his throat.

"We'll talk about your modeling career," Roger Hallen said, "and then I'll say that you're thinking about putting it all down in a book and I'll say I'm looking forward to reading it."

"Okay," Crystal said.

"And call me Roger, okay?" He had a warm smile.

"Fine, Roger."

The director cued Hallen back in just as the red light came on the camera directly facing them.

"So, what's it like being a young model—how old did you say you were?"

"Sixteen," Crystal said.

"Sixteen? They didn't make sixteen-year-old girls like you when I was sixteen!"

The audience laughed.

"And I didn't make any sixteen-year-old girls when I was sixteen, either!"

There was whistling and larger applause.

"I guess being a model can be pretty exciting?"

"It's very exciting, Roger," Crystal said. "It's like a dream come true."

"So are you." Hallen rolled his eyes toward the studio ceiling. "Let me ask you something. Be honest, now. When did you first discover you were a very beautiful girl?"

Crystal opened her mouth and nothing came out.

"Okay, let me change that." Hallen shifted his position, obviously pleased with himself. "When did the boy next door first discover he couldn't look at you and breathe normally at the same time?"

There was more applause, and Hallen laughed with the audience.

"I thought I was okay-looking last year," Crystal said.

"Okay-looking?" Hallen rolled his eyes again and there were more whistles from the audience. "There were guys all over the country slowing down their pacemakers the moment you walked out here."

"You're nice," Crystal said.

"What's absolutely the best thing about being a glamorous model?"

"I think it's seeing your pictures in print and thinking that you've done a good job," Crystal said. "It's very rewarding."

"You know, I think there are more and more opportunities for Black girls in modeling, wouldn't you say?" Hallen asked.

"I hope so," Crystal responded, remembering Loretta's admonishment not to contradict Hallen.

The rest of the interview took six minutes and Crystal found herself kissing Roger Hallen and walking off the small set to a round of applause. A moment later, the monitor showed a tiger jumping into a gas tank.

"You were wonderful!" Loretta was waiting backstage. "Absolutely wonderful!"

"That thing with the book really threw me," Crystal said.

"It worked out fine," Loretta said. "Do you know how many close-ups they had of you?"

"I was afraid to look at the monitor," Crystal said.

"Plenty," Loretta said. "Carol was in the front row. I'm sure you didn't see her, but she'll be in the lobby when we get there. I think you just turned on your afterburners, young lady. You are on your way!"

As they left, Crystal saw the assistant director offering a tissue to the author of the book Roger Hallen thought *she* had written.

12

"SHE's AT BOULEVARD HOSPITAL IN QUEENS," LORETTA said. "She asked for you but I don't think you should go. Very frankly, I think Rowena's got herself into a very bad emotional state, and I don't want you to get into one, too."

"I won't," Crystal said. "But maybe I'll drop by to see her after school."

"What time do you plan on being there?"

"I'll be out at two-thirty today," Crystal said. "I guess I can get there by three-thirty."

"You'll call me afterwards?"

"Sure."

The subway ride from Brooklyn to Boulevard Hospital was a long one. On the way, Crystal thought about getting a private tutor. It was a good idea. She knew that she was slipping way behind in her work, and she didn't know how she was going to catch up. A private tutor could work with her at home, perhaps. At any rate, it wouldn't be as embarrassing as not knowing the answers in school.

Boulevard didn't smell like some hospitals she had been in. It was clean and fresh and the nurses looked good in their crisp white outfits. There were younger girls in pink-and-white striped outfits, whom Crystal figured to be nursing assistants.

She could easily imagine herself doing that kind of work. Just helping people, not being anything special. She watched two girls talking. They were a little older than she was, maybe eighteen. They looked happy together.

"Visiting hours are not until four, it's ten minutes to four," the heavy, white-haired lady at the reception desk said. "Are you over fourteen? You have to be at least fourteen to go on the wards."

"I saw the sign," Crystal said.

"Do you have school I.D.?" the woman asked.

Crystal showed the woman her school I.D.

"Haven't I seen you someplace before?" The woman pulled her glasses to the end of her nose and peered at Crystal over them.

"I've done some modeling work," Crystal said. "You might have seen me in a magazine."

"Well, isn't that nice." The woman smiled pleasantly. "I *thought* I had seen you somewhere before!"

"I'll wait over here." Crystal started walking toward the leatherette couches.

"Oh, you can go on up," the woman said. "Your friend's in room two-twenty-seven."

There were two nurses at the reception desk on the second floor. They were watching a small television set. One of them glanced toward Crystal and beckoned her over.

"Visiting hours are— Who are you visiting?"

"Rowena," Crystal said. "I think she's in two-twenty-seven?"

"Are you a model?" The younger nurse— a tall, red-haired

163

girl with freckles that seemed concentrated around her nose—leaned forward.

"Yes," Crystal said. "How's Rowena doing?"

"She could be doing better," the red-haired nurse said to Crystal. "What kinds of things do you model for?"

"Perfume, other stuff," Crystal said.

"I'll look for your picture," the other nurse said. "You can go in now."

"What's wrong with Rowena?"

The two nurses exchanged glances. "She tried very hard to hurt herself," the older nurse said. "She cut her wrists and took some pills."

"What?"

"Are you sure you're over fourteen?" The red-haired nurse stood up.

Crystal fumbled through her bag and took out her I.D. again. She showed it to the two women.

"Don't stay too long," the red-haired nurse said. "And why don't you stop by the desk on your way out, okay?"

Crystal nodded and started down the hall. She felt nervous, almost afraid. Loretta had just said that Rowena was ill. She didn't say that Rowena had tried to kill herself.

The room was fairly large. There were two beds. The one near the door was empty. Rowena, incredibly pale, was in the other. Crystal stood in the door for a long moment, then entered. She went as quietly as she could to the bed.

Rowena's eyes were puffy, but they were open. Crystal stood near the bed. There was an I.V. going into Rowena's left arm. Both of her wrists were bandaged. On one wrist was the plastic identification bracelet all patients wore.

"Hi." Crystal spoke softly.

Rowena moved her eyes away from where Crystal stood, without moving her head.

Crystal heard a doctor being paged. The sound of the intercom seemed to come from a great distance. Traffic noises drifted from the street below.

"How are you feeling?" she asked.

"Stupid," Rowena said. "Stupid and ugly."

"You don't look ugly," Crystal said.

"Yes, I do." Rowena's voice cracked as she spoke. "I've been ugly a long time. I know that. I know that."

"That's not true," Crystal said. She put out her hand to touch Rowena's, then moved it away quickly from the bandages.

"You look at the pictures, and they say that they're okay, but you know they're ugly."

"Hey, Rowena, don't talk like that. You're going to be okay," Crystal said. She could feel the tears stinging her eyes. "Honest."

"Crystal, I feel so bad."

"Oh, baby." Crystal put her hand against Rowena's cheek. "Please get all right."

"Could you tell my mom I'm in the hospital?" Rowena asked. "Don't tell her what happened or anything, just tell her . . . tell her I'm sick. Okay?"

"Okay. Sure."

"The phone probably isn't working. We always used to have a joke, me and Mom. We'd try to figure out what worked most, Dad or the phone."

"I'll go see her," Crystal said.

165

"The name is Maria DeLea," Rowena said. "I always used to say she married my father just so her name would rhyme. But it makes it easy to remember. She lives on Bank Street in Jersey City. You can get the bus at the Port Authority. The fare's only a dollar and seventy-five. Something like that. Anyway, she's always home. She don't go out or anything."

"I'll do it," Crystal said.

"Just tell her that Rosa is sick, and see if it's all right if I can come home."

"You're Rosa?"

"Yeah. Don't tell anybody you're seeing my mom, okay?"

"How come?"

"Where I come from, my folks and all, it's not the greatest place, you know? That's why anything that happens to me in New York, in modeling, it really isn't so bad."

"I won't tell anybody," Crystal said.

"Is my face clean?" Rowena asked. "I don't have any makeup or anything on?"

"There's a little liner around your eyes," Crystal said. "You want me to make you up so you look like Rowena again?"

"No." Rowena spoke softly. "Clean it all off, so I'm Rosa again."

There were tissues near the side of the bed, and Crystal started cleaning Rowena's face. She had cream in her purse and put it on first, then wiped it carefully off.

"When you get out of here we're going to have a great time," Crystal said. "We're going to go down to M.I.S. on Forty-ninth Street and buy them out. You have a little lipstick on, too. You'd better leave it, because your lips look so dry."

"I want all of it off." Rowena's eyes were closed.

"Okay, buddy," Crystal said.

"I knew you'd come," Rowena said when Crystal had finished taking the lipstick off. "Before . . . when I was just laying in Jerry's place on the floor, I kept thinking about you. I kept thinking that I had you for my friend."

"I am your friend," Crystal said. "Now you tell me what we're going to do together when you get well again."

"I don't know," Rowena said. "Maybe just hang out?"

"Yeah, sure."

There was a footstep behind Crystal, and she turned to see Loretta come in with a short, dapper man. Crystal patted Rowena's shoulder as Loretta and the man went to the other side of the bed.

"How you doing, young lady?" Loretta asked.

"Okay," Rowena said. "I'm feeling a lot better now."

"This is Dr. Barber." Loretta touched the man's sleeve lightly. "He's an old friend and he's going to look out for you for a while."

"I'm pleased to meet such a lovely young lady," Dr. Barber said. He spoke with a slight accent. "I'm sure you are going to be just fine."

"Jerry got a call from Miller Belts," Loretta said. "They want you to do their new spring line. He told them you were busy and you'd talk to them in two weeks. You know what they did?"

"What?"

"They offered more money right away." Loretta smiled. "Jerry told them you'd definitely be in touch."

"What did they offer?" Rowena asked.

"They offered the same money for print as they did for the

spots last year," Loretta said, nodding in obvious satisfaction. "He asked me to handle the paperwork, if that's all right with you."

"That's real good." Rowena tried to force a smile. "I don't know if I'll be . . . ready in two weeks."

"You'll be ready." Loretta leaned over the bed and pushed Rowena's hair out of her eyes. "You're going to have to get out of here and control Jerry. He was talking to another account about you on the phone today. You know the Famolare account?"

"Shoes," Rowena said. "I did that last year."

"Looks like they want you back," Loretta said.

"Are you getting a lot of rest?" Dr. Barber asked. "A lot of sleep?"

"I don't sleep much," Rowena said.

"You have to get your sleep. I'm going to have a talk with the resident in half an hour," Dr. Barber said. "We'll have you back and working very shortly. Do you know that work is an excellent medicine?"

Rowena smiled.

"Look, we'd better get out of here," Loretta said. "I've got a lot of good things planned for you, a lot of hard work, so we'd better let you get your rest."

"Loretta?"

"He's got stomach problems again," Loretta said, "You know how Jerry's stomach is."

"Was he eating Chinese food?" Rowena asked. "I told him to stay away from Chinese food."

"I'll remind him." Loretta leaned over the bed and kissed

Rowena. "Meanwhile, young lady, you get some rest."

"And I'll be by in the morning to see you again," Dr. Barber said. "Loretta insists that I take personal care of you."

Loretta started toward the door. Dr. Barber moved around toward the end of the bed, looked at Rowena's chart, nodded, and left.

"Take care of yourself, baby," Crystal said.

"Okay, and don't forget to do that favor for me," Rowena said. She moved her arm and winced. Crystal kissed her on the cheek and left.

As soon as they were away from the room, Loretta took Crystal's arm and moved her quickly down the hallway, away from Rowena's room. "You've got the part!" Loretta turned Crystal around in the hall. "Joe Sidney called and said it's yours. All you have to do is show up!"

"The movie?"

"*The* movie," Loretta said. "And you're going to be *the* movie star!"

"Oh my goodness!"

"He's sending over letters of commitment in the morning. The financing is in two parts, so he needs signatures for two six-month periods. He said he saw the photos and he thinks they were great!"

"He saw the photos?"

"Jerry must have sent him a set," Loretta said. "Anyway, I want you to get everything out of your mind except this role. The movie people want to see you sometime this week to discuss a publicity strategy with you. I think he just wants to see how excited you are."

"Oh."

"You don't sound very enthusiastic. Is there something wrong?"

"No, I guess not," Crystal said.

"This thing with Rowena?"

"That a little," Crystal said.

"Look, Crystal, Dr. Barber is a psychiatrist," Loretta said. "He's going to have a go at Rowena. I think she has mental problems, and I'm going to do my best to help her out of what Dr. Barber thinks is a state of temporary depression. Then, frankly, I'm going to suggest to her that she try another business. This is a tough business to start in, and I think it's even tougher to stay in. What Rowena needs is to marry a postal worker and have lots of adorable babies."

"What happened?"

"She'd been working with one of the agencies, Sue Charney or somebody, and then she left them and Jerry's been handling her. Jerry told her she lost an account, but what really happened is he decided to drop her. That's what happens when you let a photographer represent you. He has to balance your career with his own."

"It's not fair," Crystal said.

"It's hard, Crystal. But it's fair. People have too much money tied up in these accounts to worry about everyone's problems."

"But I think Jerry and Rowena . . . you know, mean more to each other than just accounts," Crystal said. "Sometimes when she talked about him, she just seemed to light up. It's as if she's not really alive unless he's around."

"Dr. Barber, would you excuse us for a minute?" Loretta put her hand on the arm of the white-haired man. Dr. Barber nodded and walked down the hall toward the nurse's station.

"Crystal, sometimes we confuse interest and attention with love," Loretta said. "I think that Jerry was interested in Rowena, but I don't think he ever loved her."

"Does she know that?"

"Sometimes we don't want to know that we're not loved," Loretta said.

Crystal felt the tears stinging her eyes as she turned away from Loretta. She felt the older woman's arm around her waist as they walked toward where Dr. Barber waited, talking to one of the nurses.

"Do you want a lift to your hotel?" Dr. Barber asked Loretta.

"At least to Manhattan," Loretta said. "Crystal, don't get too upset over this. Rowena's very emotional, but she'll get over this. Trust me, you go home now and get some rest. Call Sue in the morning, and she'll talk to you about registering with the Screen Actors Guild."

They were in the lobby of the hospital. "By the way, what favor did Rowena want you to do for her?"

"Favor?" Crystal looked at Loretta. "Oh, to bring her some makeup."

"Don't bother," Loretta said. "I'll send some over by messenger. You know what I believe? I believe you can get sick just by visiting hospitals. Something to do with staph infections, I think. I read a study about that a few years ago."

The bus rocked and jolted its way through the tunnel to Jersey City. Crystal stared through the dirty windows at the busy, narrow streets and tried to imagine Rowena walking along them. She couldn't. It was such a distant life from modeling. She and Rowena worked in the sweaty business of making glamour, and here were the people they made it for. The bus squealed to a stop, sending an elderly man against her shoulder.

Crystal continued looking out of the window, ignoring the man's apology. A young girl—one hand gently rubbing her belly swollen from pregnancy, her large, dark eyes directed upward toward the overcast sky—sat on a graffiti-covered stoop. Two young men passed and one of them spoke to her. The girl turned away from them.

The bus driver told Crystal where to get off for the Bank Street address she had looked up in the telephone directory. It took another fifteen minutes of looking before Crystal found herself standing on a sagging porch next to an old refrigerator. It was yellow, and the bottom of the side that faced Crystal was badly rusted. A small child, his pants so low he had to keep pulling them up with one hand, played in the corner of the porch. He wore a dirty T-shirt that said SUPER on the front and HERO on the back.

Crystal knocked on the frame of the open door. The paint on the frame itself was chipped and covered with soot. Crystal thought that she might have gotten the wrong address.

"Yes?"

"Mrs. DeLea?"

"I'm Mrs. DeLea." The woman in the doorway was very

ir, with dark slits for eyes. "You from St. Al's? Father Murhy said he'd send somebody around to see me."

"No, I'm a friend of Rosa, your daughter."

"Oh." The face softened. "She's not here right now."

"I know," Crystal said. "She asked me to come here. She's little sick, and she asked me to let you know. She wants to now if she can . . ."

The words were coming slower and slower. The face of the oman in front of her was concerned, anxious. But the eyes—e eyes misted and looked away. Crystal didn't want to say nything more to her, didn't want to share this hurt with her.

"You can't come in right now," Mrs. DeLea said, softly. My husband's home and he doesn't like visitors. He's asleep, we can talk for a while. Is she bad sick?"

"Kind of," Crystal said.

The misting gave way to tears. Crystal could see the wom-n trying to pull herself together, trying to summon up rength. "I don't have much money. I think I've got twenty ollars. . . ."

"She doesn't need any money," Crystal said. "She's got oney."

"She still doing the modeling?" Mrs. DeLea asked.

"Yes." Crystal felt uncomfortable standing on the porch. he child came over to them and stood against Mrs. DeLea's gs. "I think she's going to be working again soon."

"You tell her that I hope she's okay," Mrs. DeLea said. "I ould come and see her, but I really can't get away with the aby and all."

"She wants to know if she can come home," Crystal said.

Mrs. DeLea didn't speak. She just shook her head "no" ver'
quickly.

"I think she needs to," Crystal said softly.

"My husband's very sick," Mrs. DeLea said, almost unde
her breath. "He can't stand nobody around him that don'
listen, and Rosa, she just won't listen to him. I don't wan
him to hurt her or nothing. Before, he hurt her prett'
bad."

"I'll tell her maybe she can come home later?" Crystal said
"Okay?"

"When she left, I was so scared for her." She moved he
hand to her face as she spoke. She looked tired, as if perhap
she had always been tired. "I didn't take no money from he
or nothing. She offered, because that's the kind of girl she is
That's the kind of person, you know what I mean?"

"Yes."

"I just told her to do for herself. She's young."

"I know."

"You a friend of hers?"

"Yes, we work together, too." Crystal found herself speakin
low.

"You tell her she's on my mind night and day," Mrs. DeLe
said. "You tell her she's on my mind just night and day."

"I'll tell her that," Crystal said. "You want me to tell he
you'll come to see her when you can?"

"Yeah, tell her that, too." Mrs. DeLea nodded. "I can se
you're real sweet. You know what to say."

The baby scooted into the house between her legs. Whe'
the door was closed Mrs. DeLea's face through the scree'

174

looked like the faces of women Crystal had seen in old tapestries at the museum.

13

THE NEXT DAY, LORETTA CALLED EARLY AND SAID SHE HAD set up a meeting with Joe Sidney and his publicity director.

"They want your mother to come along, too," Loretta said. "I think that's good, don't you?"

Crystal said that it probably was.

The meeting was at L'Auberge d'Hiver restaurant. Loretta wore a simple Halston but with outrageous earrings. Carol Brown wore a dress she had bought just that morning at Altman's. Loretta insisted that Crystal try the gazpacho with chilies and shrimp. The waiter suggested that they share an *Île Flottante* for dessert.

Sidney, once their luncheon had been completed, said that he thought they might shoot the entire movie in Italy or Greece.

"Perhaps in a small village near Piraeus," he said.

Across from them, two very loud people sat discussing how much money they had made that day.

Nobody mentioned Rowena.

When she got home, Crystal called the hospital, and they said that there was no change in Rowena's condition. Loretta had said that she had cosmetics sent over to Rowena but didn't see how she was going to be strong enough even to make herself up.

Crystal wanted to visit her that evening but couldn't. She didn't know what to say to Rowena about her mother. She called Jerry and told him. Jerry said that Rowena came from a rough background.

"I know," Crystal said into the phone. "But I wondered if there was anything we could do for her now."

"There probably is," Jerry said. "But I don't think we should try to figure it out. I'm paying for Dr. Barber. He's going to make an evaluation of her."

"And then?"

"Then we'll talk to her and see what goes from there."

"What do you think'll happen?"

"Crystal, I don't think it's fair of us to put ourselves in that position," Jerry said.

"By the way," she said, "what pictures did you send to Sidney?"

"The same package that Everby got," Jerry said.

"Alyce showed me some in the studio . . ."

"She showed you the bad shots," Jerry said quickly. "When I get a chance, I'll take a look at them. Look, Crystal, pictures are pictures, they don't mean anything. You're still a good girl."

"I think so," Crystal said.

"Look, I have to get into the darkroom," Jerry said. A moment later, he was saying good-bye, and the phone clicked off.

176

Crystal wondered what kind of boyfriend Jerry was. She had never had a steady boyfriend or even anyone she had liked enough to call her boyfriend. She thought of Charlie. He was tall, awkward, so far away from the rest of her life. What would he do in Greece? What would Sidney think of him?

She decided that she would go to see Rowena the next day. She would tell her what her mother had said. No, she would tell her that her mother had said she could come home later.

There was an excitement to picking up the script. Crystal had become a model accidentally and was still too new to the business to even decide if she really liked it or not. It was nice having people she had known all of her life suddenly begin to pay attention to her. It was as if she were a new person, someone they hadn't seen before. And as often as she told herself that being beautiful wasn't that important, it did make her feel good for people to say that about her.

But being in a movie was something else again. It was like being in a lovely dream in the middle of the day with the sun shining and bands playing around her. She didn't like Sidney, but it didn't matter that much. She remembered reading an interview in which an actress was telling the reporter how difficult John Huston had been.

"He's a grumpy bear of a man," the actress had said. "His only grace being his genius."

The offices of CPM Productions were on Lexington Avenue and Sixtieth Street. Crystal got there at five minutes to eleven. She had to sign in with the Spanish doorman in the lobby who phoned Joe Sidney's office on the ninth floor. She had to wait nearly ten minutes before the doorman let her up.

A young man doing his nails was seated behind the desk in the outer office.

"You're Crystal Brown?" he asked. He had a strong, masculine voice, but he was wearing eyeliner.

"Yes," she answered. "I'm supposed to pick up a script."

"You're very lovely," he said, making it sound like something other than a compliment. "I'm Tom."

Crystal responded with a nod as Tom pushed a button on the telephone set before him.

"Crystal Brown is here to see you about a script," he said into the receiver. Then he told her to go in, indicating a different office from the one she, Loretta, and her mother had been in before. There was a brass plaque on the side of the door that read SIDNEY. She tried the door; it was locked. She turned back to Tom, who flashed a saccharin grin and buzzed her through.

It looked more like a living room than an office. The entire room was done in oranges and yellows. There was a conversation pit against one wall in which two enormous couches, separated by a hideous orange rug, faced each other. The bookshelves along the walls were filled completely with orange and yellow bound books. In the middle of the room, on a platform, was what looked like a small indoor pool. To the left of the pool, seated behind a solid mahogany desk, was Joe Sidney.

"I got stock in Villeroy & Boch," Sidney said. "I had them build this little number for me."

"What is it?" Crystal asked.

"It's the biggest bathtub on the East Coast," Sidney said. "Go on up and take a look. It's got steps on the other side."

Crystal took a deep breath and walked around the tub. She stepped up on the first stair and looked in.

"It's different," Crystal said, stepping quickly down again.

"If you can't be different," Sidney said, "you're not going to make it in this world. The script is on the bookcase over there, near the lamps. One's got your name on it. Your part's highlighted in yellow. Go get it and let me hear you read."

Crystal felt herself tense. She hadn't thought about reading for the part. She went to where Sidney had indicated and saw a pile of scripts. She thumbed through each one until she found the one with KRISTAL printed on it. She wondered if Tom had done that.

She went over to the couch and opened the script to the first page that had dialogue for her. She began to read aloud.

"'This might be the worst vacation I've ever had.'"

"You're supposed to be from Spain, but I think we're going to make that Marrakesh," Sidney said. "I know we're going to change your name. Something with an 'e' sound on the end. That sounds more exotic. You want to try the hot tub? Some people find it very relaxing."

"No, thank you." Crystal smiled. She thought of what Loretta had said, about smiling when she didn't feel like it.

"Keep reading." Sidney was stuffing papers into a dark leather briefcase.

"'Oh, Eduardo, you're so silly. Why shouldn't you love me? What are human beings made for, if not to love each other?'"

Crystal read the part slowly.

"'It's not the idea of loving you. It's why should you love me. After all, I'm nothing but a dishwasher in this hotel,'" Sidney had the part memorized.

"Are you going to play that role?" Crystal asked.

"No, but I know all the parts," Sidney said. "I could recite yours if I wanted to. Look, are you comfortable standing over there?"

"Not really," Crystal said.

"Why don't you take your clothes off and get into the tub?" Sidney said.

"No, thank you," Crystal said, hoping that he had noticed the edge in her voice.

"Keep reading." Sidney's voice changed noticeably. Crystal looked for where she had stopped reading.

"'You mean that somebody would find out about us?'" Crystal read.

"'Heavens no,'" Sidney droned on. "'The pain of losing you. And I know that eventually I must. As soon as I become, you know, serious.'"

"'Don't be silly! I want you to be serious, Eduardo.'"

"You know what business this is, Crystal?" Sidney stood and walked around the desk. "This ain't the beauty business, it's the being young business."

"'I don't think I could ever live without you.'" Crystal continued reading her part.

"You're hot stuff because you're young stuff," Sidney said. "Don't forget that. Young flesh is always exciting, and the world is full of young flesh."

"'My only problem, Eduardo, is that I want to get married.'"

"Okay, okay. Look, I'm headed downtown," Sidney said. "Bring the script and I'll drop you off. Keep reading."

"Am I reading the part all right?" Crystal asked.

"Yeah, I can understand the words," Sidney said. He started out the door and Crystal followed, reading as she went. Sidney told Tom to call for his car. Crystal read the part that he had interrupted.

"How come you read that part twice?" Sidney asked.

"I thought you didn't hear me," Crystal replied.

"Go on, go on." He nodded at her. Then, even before she started, he called to Tom not to take any calls from somebody named Lucy Libreman. "She's a mystery writer. I borrowed a few ideas from her and now she wants to sue me."

"'Of course, it doesn't make any difference that you're just a dishwasher. I love you for your personality, not your job.'"

Crystal nodded toward two young girls in the elevator. She held up the script so that they could see it.

By the time they reached the sidewalk, the car was in front. The doorman opened the door and Sidney got in. He motioned to Crystal to get in, and she went around the front of the car, barely being missed by a delivery boy on a three-wheeled contraption.

"Where are we going?" Crystal asked.

"I'm headed toward my place," Sidney said. "I'll give you cab money to get to . . . where are you from, Brooklyn?"

"Brooklyn," Crystal said.

She continued reading. Sidney drove fast and expertly. Now and again he corrected her reading of the script. On Tenth Street and Fifth Avenue, at a stoplight, he told her to reach into the glove compartment and take out a card.

Crystal looked at the card. It had Joe Sidney's name and address on it. She was looking at it when he put his hand on her leg.

"Don't!" she said.

"What do you mean, *don't*?" Sidney asked. "You see me and you see you, right?"

"I just don't want your hands on me," Crystal said. The light changed and the car started moving forward.

"Don't give me that crap," Sidney said. "You just tell me one thing. Do you see me and do you see you?"

"Yes, of course I do."

"And what you should see when you see me is a guy who can make you a friggin' movie star. And what you should see when you see you is just another pretty puss that can't make nothing without me turning you on to the movies. Why you think Loretta's pushing so hard for this? Huh? She's pushing hard because she don't think you're gonna make her any money without a movie. She didn't tell you that?"

"She said something like that," Crystal said.

"Damn straight!" Joe Sidney put his hand on Crystal's leg. "We're going to my place."

They drove on toward Bedford Street. Crystal didn't move. Joe Sidney's hand on her leg was the heaviest thing she had ever felt. She started to pretend that it wasn't her in the car. It wasn't her, just someone, a girl, riding in a car. A girl she hardly knew.

"So what do you think?" Joe Sidney smiled and chewed on the unlit cigar in his mouth. "I'm not such a bad guy after all, eh?"

182

The car was stopped. Crystal looked up. She pushed Sidney's hand away as hard as she could and opened the door just as he started the car up. He slammed on the brake, sending her arm into the dashboard.

"What the hell's wrong with you?" he shouted at her. "You high or something?"

An old lady walking a Pekingese watched as Crystal half jumped, half stumbled out of Sidney's car. The woman pulled the dog's leash toward her and lifted him into her arms as Sidney reached over and slammed the door shut. He started up again, brought the car to a squealing halt, and backed up to where Crystal still stood at the curb. He threw something from the car that landed near her feet.

"Pick it up!" he shouted, angrily.

Crystal picked up the script and clutched it in her hands as Sidney's car lurched forward and down the busy street.

"Young lady, I don't know where you live," the old woman said haughtily. "But we don't allow that sort of thing in this neighborhood!"

14

IT WASN'T SO MUCH WHAT JOE SIDNEY HAD DONE AS IT was what he had said. "Do you see me and do you see you?" he had asked. "And what you should see when you see you is just another pretty puss . . ." And it was the grin, the grin that said that he knew everything that was going to be. That he knew everything about her. Crystal looked up and saw the traffic flashing by. There were a few older women looking at her from the corner.

She looked for a subway. She would go to the hospital and tell Rowena about Joe Sidney. Rowena would laugh. They would be girls again, not models, not even beautiful or sexy, just girls.

Rowena had asked her if she wanted to be friends, and it hadn't meant very much to her then. Now it did. Now it meant that there was someone to talk to who would know how she felt. She would tell her about Joe Sidney. She would tell her how stupid he looked with his big cigar dangling from his mouth. How mad he had been when Crystal had opened the car door to get out.

Crystal imagined what Rowena would say about Sidney. She would laugh at him, but knowing Rowena, she would find a way to like him. Crystal clutched the script tighter under her arm and wondered if she would find a way of liking him, too.

The "E" train rattled through the tunnel, jerking the faceless passengers from side to side as it raced crosstown through Manhattan toward Queens. The crowd thinned out at Lexington and again at Ely Avenue. Crystal tried not to think. She read the ad cards over the seats. One card advertised Preparation H in Spanish. The card next to it, in English, showed a girl's rear end lifted high in a pair of jeans. She thought she recognized the girl. She looked closely. It was one of the girls she had worked with before. She had a dark wig on and earrings that hung almost to her shoulders.

Crystal changed trains and took the "GG" to her stop.

"Rowena," she said.

The white-haired volunteer flipped through a patient card index and announced that they didn't have a Rowena.

"That's that model the guys from housekeeping were talking about." Another white-haired volunteer flipped through the cards. "I don't see her card here, but she's listed as DeLea, something like that. Are you a model, honey?"

Crystal nodded.

"You're very pretty," the woman said. The magic words. "Why don't you go right up."

Crystal started for the elevator. Behind her, one of the ladies said something about "them" using a lot of colored models. A small boy on the elevator peeked around his mother and smiled at Crystal, and Crystal smiled back.

"My father broke his arm," the boy said. The mother smiled.

"I'm sorry to hear that," Crystal replied.

"He was drunk," the boy said.

The mother's face hardened instantly. She pushed the boy behind her and looked at Crystal with instant hate. Crystal looked away.

"May I help you?" said a candy striper, a bit overweight with a soft neck that ran into her chin. She would look terrible on television, Crystal thought.

"Rowena?" Crystal pointed toward Rowena's room.

"Oh!" The girl turned to the nurse on duty.

"You're a friend of hers, aren't you?" It was the red-haired nurse from before.

"Yes, how's she doing?" Crystal asked.

"I'm afraid we have some rather bad news for you." The nurse came around the counter. Her large blue eyes found Crystal's and held them.

"Rowena?"

"Could you get us some coffee?" The nurse spoke, moving her head ever so slightly toward the candy striper to indicate to whom she was speaking.

She took Crystal by the shoulders and led her into a small room. Another nurse was doing a crossword puzzle at the table. She got up and walked silently away.

"She just seemed to give up," the nurse said.

"Did anything happen?" Crystal heard herself stammering. "What . . . ?"

"I don't know what happened," the nurse said. "I'm so sorry."

Rowena dead?

"But I just spoke to her yesterday!" Crystal's voice broke as she spoke. "It was just about . . ." She looked at the clock over the file cabinet. The face of the clock broke up through her tears. The hands moved in uneven orbits.

"Here's the coffee." The candy striper put two cups on the table.

Crystal looked at the girl, who was probably a year or two older than she was. The girl tried to force a smile and then turned away.

Crystal cried. Her shoulders shook with the sobs and her eyes burned with the tears. The nurse held her tightly, squeezing her shoulders as if she were going to squeeze every bit of sorrow from her.

186

The wind lifted bits of paper from the sidewalk and flung them against her legs outside of the hospital. Where would Rowena be? Crystal remembered *Quincy*, the television show. Rowena would be in some cold room. There would be conversations going on about her that she could not hear. There would be lights glaring down at her. She would be still. Her face not made up. Rosa, at the last.

Tears. Crystal leaning against the dark-brick corner of the hospital. A policeman stood on the sidewalk not far from her. He looked at his watch and turned away.

She went into the subway. For a moment, she was confused. The nurse had asked her to stay until her mother could come. But what would her mother have said? That it was a shame? That she couldn't dwell on what had happened to Rowena?

Where was she? That was the important thing. Where was she?

Crystal looked into her pocketbook. She had twenty dollars in her wallet and fifteen dollars in her pockets. Where would she go?

She wanted to run home and tell her father. She wanted to say "Daddy, Rowena is dead."

"Dead?" he would say. He would look at her and his forehead would move. He would search her face. Maybe he would lift her chin. "Who's Rowena?" he would ask.

"A model," she would say. "A model like me."

"How she die?"

"She tried to kill herself," Crystal would say. "And then just gave up trying to live."

"Why?" he would ask.

He would ask why, and she knew he wouldn't be thinking

about Rowena. He would be thinking about her.

"I don't know, Daddy," she would say. "I just don't know."

Then he would grab a beer and storm around the house, dark and brooding. It was his way. He would pound the walls with his fists and with his eyes flashing the anger he felt.

She would feel sorry for her father. Sorry for his anger and his frustration. But it would be her mother, sitting in the kitchen, her face tightened in the shadows, who would say the things that would push Crystal on to the next day.

"If you have a chance, honey," she would say, "you have to take it. We're like people drowning in our own history. We can't turn down our chances when they come."

Her lips would find words of sorrow for Rowena, and then they would say that Rowena was Rowena and Crystal was Crystal. It wasn't where she had come from, it wasn't her history that had failed Rowena, it was the "look" that she had lost. She should have had her eyes fixed. Maybe, even, gone to Europe.

Crystal thought of going to Rowena's mother's house. She would go there and knock on the door. But then there would be nothing to say. Just pain to be rolled around the mouth and offered through lips lined with a shade slightly lighter than her lipstick to make her lips appear less full.

Crystal stopped at a phone booth and called home. The phone rang several times before she heard her mother's voice announcing that it was the Browns' residence.

"Rowena's dead, Mommy."

"I know, honey," her mother answered softly. "Loretta

alled earlier and told me. She suggested that we might all get
ogether for dinner tonight. Of course, your father won't be
ble to make it."

"I saw Joe Sidney—"

"Yes, Loretta said he called her." Her mother's voice raised
a tone the way it did sometimes when she was excited. "He
aid you read for the part very well. Loretta thinks he must
ave got the money. Are you on your way home now?"

"Not yet," Crystal said. "I have something to do first.
hen I'll be home."

"Loretta was thinking about dinner between seven-thirty
nd eight. . . ." Her mother's voice trailed off.

"I'll try to make it by then," Crystal said.

She hung up the phone, hung on to the receiver for support
r a long moment, then dropped in another quarter. She
ade another phone call, then hailed a cab.

The driver had asked her three times if she had the money
r the cab ride from Queens into Manhattan. Crystal knew it
as the crying. No matter how hard she tried, she couldn't
op the flow of tears or her shoulders from shaking. The driver
as angry. When they reached the address on Bedford Street
at Crystal had given him, he jerked the cab to a halt.

"That'll be fourteen-forty!" he said.

Crystal took a twenty-dollar bill from her wallet and gave it
 the driver. He looked at the twenty and at her as she left the
ab. He called out his thanks. Crystal wasn't interested.

The stairs to the brownstone were spotless, no graffiti
arred them. The brass fixtures at the door were polished and

189

the black grillwork freshly painted. Crystal looked at the address on the script. The top of the two addresses was Joe Sidney's office. The bottom was his home.

"Come in." He stepped away from the door.

Crystal entered.

"I thought you would change your mind," he said. "You gotta be smart in this business and you impress me as nobody's dummy."

"I've made up my mind," Crystal said.

"Sure, that's why you're here," Sidney said. "Look, why don't you go into the bathroom and fix yourself up. You look a mess. I'll make us a couple of drinks. We can relax."

"I don't drink," Crystal replied.

"Whatever." Sidney took a cut-glass bottle of Scotch from the bookshelf. "The bathroom's over there. Make yourself look nice, honey. You know how to do it."

"I don't want the part," Crystal said. She didn't want to cry again, either, but the tears came. "I want to give you back your script and then it's over."

"What are you talking about?" Sidney downed his drink and poured another one.

"I've made up my mind."

"You're upset," Sidney said. "Get Loretta on the phone. Come on, hurry up! Get that agent of yours on the phone!"

Crystal had planned to say that she didn't like what she had to do or who she had become. She wanted to say something about Rowena, that the girl she had come to know, whom she had walked down the street with, whose mother she had visited, wasn't just a "look" that had passed. She was more than pretty face, or a sexy look, or something that made clothes look good or men feel good. And so was she, Crystal.

But none of the words came, and she stood in front of Joe Sidney, the tears streaming down her face, leaving streak marks where they ran over her foundation.

"Look, we've got a commitment." Joe Sidney put down the drink. "We're going to Italy, we're going to make a film; and you're going to be a star in spite of yourself! Now—"

Crystal turned away and started toward the door. Sidney got to it first and slammed the palm of his hand across the carved panel.

"You can throw your career away if you want to," he said, his face reddening with anger, "but you're not throwing my living away in the process! You don't have to come across if you don't want to, but you *are* making the movie. I've got the money in place and you *are* making the movie."

Crystal ran the back of her hand under her nose and tried to pull Joe Sidney's hand away. She couldn't budge it. She looked into his face. He was smiling.

"Please let me out."

"Look, no one is going to hurt you," he said softly. "Why don't we just sit down and talk about this whole thing? Now doesn't that sound more reasonable than you standing in the middle of the floor crying your friggin' eyes out?"

The doorbell rang.

"That's my friend," Crystal said.

"You told somebody to come here?" Sidney looked at her.

"I told her if I wasn't out of here in five minutes after she got here to call the police!"

Sidney looked at her. His face calmed; he shrugged.

"So leave," he said. "But this is going to be one of those moments you're going to remember, girly."

Crystal opened the door that led into the vestibule. She could feel Joe Sidney behind her.

"This is one of those moments that you're going to look back on when you're working in some fast-food joint!"

The words followed her out of the front door and down the steps as she went past Sister Gibbs.

"Crystal!" Sister Gibbs caught up with her on the street. "Are you okay, baby?"

"I'm fine, Sister Gibbs."

"That fool didn't touch you, did he?"

"No. I just made up my mind about something, and he didn't like the way I made it up."

Sister Gibbs turned back toward the well-kept brownstone in time to see Joe Sidney close the door.

"Who that man, anyway?"

"He's the one that wants me to make a film in Italy."

"You don't think we should call the police or nothing?" she asked.

"No," Crystal said, taking Sister Gibbs' hand. "And thanks for coming."

"Girl, when you call me and tell me to meet you over in this neighborhood because you need somebody to be with, I was worried sick," Sister Gibbs said as they started toward the avenue. "Just look how I run out the house looking!"

"You look just fine, Sister Gibbs," Crystal said as she took the older woman's arm. "Just fine."

192

They were sitting at the kitchen table. Carol Brown was in a housecoat, balancing a cup of coffee on her upturned palm. Crystal sat opposite her father.

"I need you to tell me about this," her father said, "and I need you to tell me what you want to do. I've been telling myself that I didn't understand your opportunities and I didn't want to mess anything up. Now, I still don't know everything that's involved in this business, but I don't have to. I see you're not happy in it. Any time you got to call Sister Gibbs instead of one of your folks, things ain't right."

"I just thank God that you're all right," Carol Brown began. "I should have realized that she needed more help with the pressures. I should have realized it."

"We didn't know it because we didn't want to know it," her father said. "All this stuff about me not standing in the way. I can't believe I let myself go for that crap."

"Daddy, please don't fight," Crystal begged.

"I'm not fighting, honey," he said. "But I'm going to be right here in the middle of everything from now on. I'm gonna sleep with both my eyes open."

"I think Crystal can use some sleep," Carol said. "And you and I can talk."

"I don't want to talk to you" was the quick answer. "I need to talk to my daughter."

"Daddy, are you going to get mad?" Crystal asked.

"I might," he said. "But I can handle it."

Crystal began to tell her father about the modeling. About how she had liked it at first and then how it had become something different.

"How did it change?"

"I don't know," she said. "Maybe it didn't even change. I was supposed to be pretty, and I was supposed to be a little sexy, I guess. It was like there were two of me. A real me underneath and an outside me that was pretty and sexy. Then after a while, the outside part just seemed to get more and more important until it was the only thing that mattered."

"You don't have to be pretty, or sexy, or anything else in the world that you don't want to be," her father said.

Carol Brown put the coffee cup down and left the room.

"Is Mama going to be all right?" Crystal asked.

"Sure, she's strong," Daniel said.

"You're not going to fight with her, are you?"

"No, I don't think so," Daniel said. "I can see where she's coming from. Sometimes, if you miss a few things along the way, you lose your perspective. She don't mean nothing but the best for you, honey. Just that sometimes the best is hard to get to. We'll get over this thing the same way we've got over a lot of other things. I ain't saying it'll be easy, because what got us here didn't happen overnight. But we'll get there."

Crystal put her arm around her father and kissed him.

15

IT WAS SOMETHING THAT CRYSTAL HAD TO DO. SHE wasn't sure what Jerry would say or do. She had just called him and said that she would be over later to talk about the pictures he had of Rowena. She started to ask her father to come with her but decided against it. She was going to ask Jerry for Rowena's pictures, the ones she had seen in the studio. She didn't want her father to know about them.

She had been so close to him the last few days. He had spent so much time showing his love for her, and for her mother, that Crystal couldn't bear to hurt him. It might come someday, she knew, but not now.

"Hi, come in." Jerry backed away from the door. He smelled vaguely like the chemicals he used in the darkroom.

"How've you been?" she asked.

"Crystal, let me show you something," Jerry said, ignoring her asking about his health.

Jerry went to the fireplace and took an envelope off the mantelpiece. He handed it to Crystal.

Crystal opened it and took out the papers inside. They were release forms that Rowena had signed.

"I figured she had signed these," Crystal said. "I'm just here to beg for them. I'm not trying anything legal. I'm just trying to get my friend's pictures back."

"You really want them?" Jerry asked.

"I really want them."

Jerry went to his desk, picked up some forms, and handed them to her. "I don't have release forms for your pictures," he said.

"Loretta said *La Femme* didn't want them, since I'm not going to be in the movie," Crystal said.

"Yeah, she told me," Jerry said. "She said you've decided

to get out of the business. You've turned down the movie, your accounts, the whole ball game. I'm sorry to hear that. But I'm still in the business."

Crystal looked at the forms. "You're saying that if I sign these you'll give me Rowena's pictures?"

"You either want them or you don't."

Crystal sat down. She looked at the release forms and up at Jerry. She hadn't even realized that she hadn't signed the forms before, but now, now that she knew, life was hard again.

She thought about Rowena lying in the hospital bed. She had asked Crystal to take her makeup off. She had wanted to be Rosa again. Her hands had been bandaged, the intravenous tube in one arm. She had been unable to help herself.

"My father doesn't read girly magazines," she said as she signed the release forms. "I just hope that his friends don't."

Jerry took the forms from her. "Wait here."

He went upstairs to his studio. Crystal looked again at the forms he had shown her. There it was, in black and white, Rowena's signing away of her life. It was a matter of minutes before she heard Jerry's footsteps on the stairs. He brought the pictures down. There were even more than she had seen before. Jerry handed Crystal a large envelope to carry the pictures in.

"You don't have to believe this," Jerry said, "but I wasn't going to sell them."

"Fine," Crystal said, standing. She pushed the pictures into the envelope and started toward the door.

"Here, take these with you, too," Jerry said. "I cared for Rowena, too, Crystal. I really did."

Crystal looked at the release forms she had just signed and pushed them into the envelope.

It was cold outside, snow flurries came down in frantic circles and melted instantly against the hard concrete. Down the street from Jerry's studio, there was an empty lot. In one corner of it, there were some men standing around a fire in a barrel. Crystal headed toward it. She smiled at the men as she dropped the pictures into the flames.

Crystal and Pat stood in front of the Regency State and looked at the pictures advertising *To Touch the Sunset*.

"We can see the movie, then we can go on over to Bloomingdale's and window-shop," Pat was saying.

"Don't you ever get tired of window-shopping at Bloomingdale's?" Crystal asked. "I mean, why don't we give some of the other stores a break? Let's go up to Tiffany's."

"I tell you what," Pat said. "I'll go to Tiffany's if we go for Chinese food afterwards."

"It's a deal, but I don't want to go see the movie," Crystal said. "The reviews were terrible."

"But they said Alyce Winslow was a knockout, and she's the only model besides you I know anything about," Pat said. "And you know the producer, right?"

"Actress now," Crystal said. "She's just doing acting now." She was looking at the stills of Alyce in a bathing suit, next to the male lead.

"You don't even want to see if she really takes off all of her clothes like they said?" Pat asked.

"She told me that she did," Crystal said. "I told you she calls me once in a while."

"You ever figure out why?" Pat asked as they started away from the marquee. "I mean, you said you were more friendly with that other girl, weren't you?"

"I was," Crystal said, "but Alyce is okay, too. It's just taking her a while."

"Okay, chummie, if you say so," Pat said. "So it's off to Tiffany's."

"Excuse me." A tall, thin man came up to the two girls. He gave Crystal his card. It said, "Edward Abruzzi, Photographer."

"You talking to us?" Crystal asked.

"Yes. You know, I think you could get into modeling," he said. "I'd even be willing to take a few shots of you on speculation if you're interested."

"Do you really think she could?" Pat asked, wide-eyed. "Can we give you a call sometime?"

"Yeah," the guy said, starting to cross the street. "If you're willing to take the business seriously, you might be able to make it. You've got the basic equipment. Give me a call during the week."

Pat dropped the card in the wastebasket as Abruzzi jumped out of the way of a cab. Then the two girls, arm in arm, began walking along the crowded New York streets toward Tiffany's.